D0793855

Amanda Grange lives in Cheshire and has had two novels published.

THE SIX-MONTH MARRIAGE

Unless Philip, Lord Pemberton, could arrange a six-month marriage he would lose his inheritance. But how could he find a respectable young lady to go along with such a scheme? Coincidentally, Madeline Delaware was desperate to escape from her dissolute uncle, so what better solution could there be? But the six-month marriage turned out to be far from the peaceful interlude that she had envisaged. And why, when the marriage was simply a convenient arrangement, did Madeline find it so difficult to think of its end?

AMANDA GRANGE

THE SIX-MONTH MARRIAGE

Complete and Unabridged

ULVERSCROFT
Leicester

First published in Great Britain in 2002 by
Robert Hale Limited
London

First Large Print Edition
published 2003
by arrangement with
Robert Hale Limited
London

British Library CIP Data

Grange, Amanda
    The six-month marriage.—Large print ed.—
Ulverscroft large print series: romance
1. Love stories
2. Large type books
I. Title
823.9'2 [F]

ISBN 0–7089–4843–X

Published by
F. A. Thorpe (Publishing)
Anstey, Leicestershire

Set by Words & Graphics Ltd.
Anstey, Leicestershire
Printed and bound in Great Britain by
T. J. International Ltd., Padstow, Cornwall

This book is printed on acid-free paper

1

'There, there.' Madeline Delaware soothed her tearful maid. 'It's all right, Jenny, really it is.' Her haunted eyes belied her words, but she did what she could to comfort the young girl. 'Come. Best get it over with.'

'What can he be thinking of?' sobbed Jenny as she applied a touch of carmine to Madeline's lips.

'I don't know,' said Madeline. She was seated at her dressing-table in a large and gloomy bedroom at the back of a run-down house in Grosvenor Square. Outside, the last light of a summer day in the year of 1813 lingered, but inside it was gloomy. Dark-gold paint covered the walls and heavy brocade curtains covered the windows. Everything about the room was oppressive, and as Madeline regarded herself in the looking-glass she was close to tears. Her face was painted with powder and rouge, and for two pins she would have washed it off, but if she did so her guardian would make her suffer for it; as well as, most likely, dismissing Jenny.

Her eyes dropped to her crimson gown. Its bodice was indecently low. She did what she

1

could to tug it higher and tried to pull the transparent sleeves back on to her shoulder, but they had been designed to fall away. She had pleaded with her guardian, her Uncle Gareth, to be allowed to wear one of her more suitable gowns, but he had refused to listen.

'Oh, miss, you have to get away from him,' sniffed Jenny. 'Before something truly dreadful happens.'

'I know,' said Madeline. 'But everywhere I go I am watched. No matter where I am — in the drawing-room, the music room, the library, wherever — Miss Handley is always there.'

'She calls herself your chaperon,' said Jenny, biting her lip. 'She's more like your gaoler.'

Madeline nodded. 'And if ever she cannot be with me there is always someone else: a maid pretending to dust the piano, a footman with a spurious message, or the housekeeper making a show of asking my advice about what to serve for dinner.'

'When you go riding . . . ' Jenny began.

Madeline shook her head. 'When I go out riding it is worse. As well as Miss Handley I am accompanied by a footman and a groom. Gareth is determined that I shall not escape.'

No matter how hard she fought against it, a

feeling of hopelessness was gradually over-taking her. Seven months of Gareth Delaware's guardianship had worn her down, making her anxious and afraid. She was confined at every turn, made a prisoner of, and denied any contact with anyone who might help her. Gareth's conduct thus far had been limited to criticizing and under-mining her, and restricting her movements so that she had had no chance to ask for help from anyone outside Delaware House. But looking at the dress she had been forced to wear she feared that things were about to get worse. Now that her twenty-first birthday was fast approaching, Gareth had decided to arrange her future. And the future he had lined up for her was one which filled her with dread.

* * *

'I don't understand you, Gareth,' she said some half an hour later, as the Delaware carriage rattled its way through the streets towards Drury Lane. It was a rare outing for Madeline, and she wondered why her uncle had decided to take her to the theatre. 'We will be cut by all our acquaintance if they see me like this. Let me go home and put on something more suitable. The white satin is just the thing for this evening. You told me not three months ago that it was the sort of gown a young lady should be wearing.'

Gareth Delaware leered at her as he lolled against the shabby squabs. Madeline gave a shudder. She did not know how it was, but Gareth always managed to look dissolute, even though his linen was clean and his breeches and tail-coat were in the height of fashion.

'You're a woman. You're not here to understand me, you're here to shut up and do as you're told. The white satin's no good tonight. I need you to get noticed, and that gown'll do the trick. It'll be the making of me. And if I don't miss my guess it'll be the making of you, too.'

Madeline shuddered again.

'We'll have none of those missish ways tonight,' he said, his voice sharpening. 'You're going to get me out of a tight corner, or it'll be the worse for you.'

'You surely can't expect any man of quality to offer for me looking like this,' she flared. Her anger gave her the courage to stand up to him. 'You have turned me into a . . . ' She couldn't bear to say the word. 'No decent man will come near me.'

Gareth only leered more. 'Spirit. I like that in a woman. And so does the Honourable

4

Lucius Spalding. It'll make you all the more fun to break in.'

Madeline's stomach contracted. 'You can't be serious, Gareth? You wouldn't marry me to Lucius Spalding?' She thought of Lucius's slack features and his licentious behaviour, and she blanched. 'You don't need to do this,' she said. 'If you are in debt to Lucius Spalding you can *have* my dowry. Only let me go and live quietly in the country and I will make no claim on it.'

Gareth laughed without humour. 'If only I could. My bloody brother — your father, my dear — tied the money up so tight there's no other way I can get to it. So if Spalding wants the ten thousand I owe him he'll have to marry you in order to get it.' He gave another leer. 'But seeing you like that, he just might decide it's not such a bad bargain after all.'

'No, Gareth, there has to be a better way.' She made one last desperate appeal to his better nature — if, indeed, he had one.

'Enough! You'll please Lucius Spalding tonight, and by God! you'll make him think you're worth taking along with your dowry, or — '

'Or what?' demanded Madeline.

A cruel smile crossed Gareth's face. 'Or we'll see what a week of being locked in your room will do.'

She would have thought his words were melodramatic if she had not known from experience that he would carry out his threat. As her legal guardian he was entitled to treat her in almost any way he chose, and, being necessarily weaker than he, she could not do a thing to stop him.

She shivered, remembering the times when he had locked her in her room before. The first time had been shortly after her arrival at Grosvenor Square, when he had invited a few friends round to dinner. He had told her she must join them, adding, 'And make sure you're nice to them'. She had thought he meant she should be polite, but had soon discovered that he meant her to flirt with them, laughing at their insults and encouraging their advances. She had left the room angrily and gone to her bedroom, only to find herself locked in for almost a week. That incident had not had the desired effect of breaking her spirit, but it had taught her one important lesson: it was better not to cross Gareth. At least not outwardly.

Inwardly, it was a different matter. Because she was not going to be forced into a marriage with Lucius Spalding. Not at any cost.

The carriage began to slow. Up ahead, hansoms and private carriages were queuing up, waiting to drop off their occupants at the theatre. Madeline hoped for a brief moment that, once she was out of the carriage, she might be able to lose herself in the crowd which spilled across the pavement and make good her escape. It was a desperate hope, but it was all she had. As the carriage rolled to a halt, however, she saw that Miss Handley was already there, waiting outside the theatre. Madeline had no choice but to step out of the carriage, and Miss Handley immediately came forward to stand guard over her. She was hemmed in, with Miss Handley in front of her and her uncle behind. She looked to left and right. There were people converging on the theatre from every direction, but it would be impossible for her to get away without her uncle and Miss Handley hauling her back, and she was forced to go in.

Inside, it was already crowded. The foyer was full of people, all laughing and chattering. The ladies, their eyes bright with enjoyment, reminded Madeline of a flock of exotic birds: their gowns of silk and satin glowed in the candlelight, and their feathered headdresses bobbed and swayed as they spoke. The gentlemen, too, were splendid. They were dressed in dark tail-coats and coloured waistcoats, or in dashing scarlet uniforms which were heavily decorated with gold braid. But Madeline could not enjoy the sight. Her mind was taken up by the thought that if she did not manage to escape from her uncle then she would be forced into a marriage with the licentious Lucius Spalding; and she knew that if she could find any way of avoiding such a dreadful fate she must take it.

Miss Handley and her uncle ushered her over to the stairs. From their conversation it soon became obvious that the three of them were due to share a box with Lucius Spalding. Perhaps he would not agree to her uncle's plan, she thought with a brief return of hope. But even if he didn't, she knew it would not be long before her uncle landed himself in debt again and tried to use her and her dowry to buy his way out of it.

Could she escape from the house once they returned home? she wondered, turning the faint hope over in her mind. The doors and windows were always kept heavily locked, but with Jenny's help she might be able to get the keys. It would be difficult, but she must try something.

'Look out! She's fainted.'

The exclamation cut into Madeline's thoughts. She looked up and saw that, at the top of the stairs, a young lady had collapsed.

'Give her air! She needs room to breathe!' came another cry.

The crowd responded to the plea, and a wave of bodies pressed back down the stairs, leaving a circle of space round the prostrate young lady. Madeline, pushed backwards by the crowd, found herself separated from the rest of her party and carried towards the door.

Her hopes began to rise. Could she . . . ? Almost without thinking she picked up her skirts and slipped through the crush of people, making for the outside. At every moment she expected to feel her uncle's hand on her arm, or Miss Handley's grip on her shoulder, but nothing came, and when she passed through the door and felt the night air on her face she knew that if she could only elude them for a few minutes, then she had a real chance of escape.

She looked both ways. Which way to go? There was no time to stop and think. She must put as much distance between her and the theatre as she could, and do it as quickly as possible. She turned and ran to the left, threading her way through the elegantly dressed people who were making their way to the theatre. Their faces were alight with pleasure as they anticipated the joys of the play to come. They gave her strange looks as she ran past and between them, but then shrugged and turned their attention back to their own business.

Madeline turned a corner and breathed more easily. Now that she was out of sight of the door her uncle, when he followed her, would either have to waste time questioning the theatre-goers, asking if they had seen her, or else he would have to send Miss Handley one way whilst he himself took another. But the further away Madeline managed to go the less her chance of recapture would be, and after taking a minute to catch her breath she went on.

The streets around the theatre were becoming darker and less frequented. The brightly lit thoroughfares gave way to less reputable streets, where shops and ale-houses seemed to crowd in on her. She began to feel vulnerable, but there was no going back. She hurried now down one street and now down another, turning at random, going wherever it seemed safest. She passed a number of gaudily dressed women — prostitutes, she guessed, having seen their like at her uncle's house — who gave her curious glances and passed a few ribald remarks, but, to her relief, she was not molested. She turned another corner and stopped, panting, to give herself a rest.

She used the time to think about what she was going to do next. If she could just get through the night, then in the morning she could try and find somewhere to sell, or at least pawn, her bracelet. It had been her mother's and she did not want to part with it, but with the money raised she could rent a room and live safely for a while until she could decide what to do next. She had no relatives to turn to, and Gareth had made sure she had not had the opportunity to make any friends, but that did not mean that she was helpless. She was young and in good health. She could earn her living if she set her mind to it, she was sure.

That settled, she turned her attention to her present predicament. She looked around her, trying to get her bearings. She had been out in the carriage with Miss Handley once or twice since arriving in London — her uncle had thought it wise to show her off now and again, when ugly rumours about his treatment of her had started to circulate — but she found that she did not recognize any of the streets or houses around her. As she stood quietly, breathing in deep draughts of the night air, a hansom drew to a halt in front of her. Madeline eyed it warily, and took a step back as a group of young bloods poured out.

'Well, well, well. Lookee at what we have here,' said one, as his eye fell on Madeline. From the way he slurred his speech it was obvious he was in his cups. 'As pretty a bit of muslin as I've ever seen. And ripe for the plucking, eh, boys?' he asked.

The men laughed and Madeline backed away.

'Seems to me you're in need of a protector, my pretty one,' said another, swaggering towards her with an unsteady gait. 'Someone who can take care of you and *look after* you, if you take my meaning,' he leered.

Madeline was still out of breath from her exertions, but she had no choice: she turned and ran down the street. Only to find that her way was blocked by another gentleman. He was tall, with a lean, rangy body. His caped greatcoat reached down to his ankles. Beneath it she caught a glimpse of his firm body encased in a blue tail-coat and a pair of cream breeches. His hair was dark, his eyes amber, and across one cheek ran a scar.

A soldier, she thought briefly.

But still a man.

Knowing from experience that men were not to be trusted she hesitated for only a moment before stepping aside, hoping to pass him. But he reached out his hand and caught her wrist.

'Find some other sport, boys,' he said, his eyes running assessingly over the three drunks who had followed her down the street. 'This ladybird's mine.'

And then, as if to underline his words, he pulled her towards him. His eyes looked down into her own; he crushed her tightly against him; and then he lifted her face up to his.

Dear God! thought Madeline. Have I left one danger behind only to find another? She felt a rising tide of panic and tried to pull away, but he had a grip of iron and she was helpless to resist. His mouth covered hers . . . and suddenly everything changed. She felt as though her bones were turning to water and a cascade of tingles, like a waterfall, ran down her spine. Her fists, which had been raised to his shoulders to push him away, uncurled, and her fingers pressed themselves against the capes of his coat. It was the most strangely delicious feeling. Her whole body became light. She felt as though she might float away; except that his strong arms were holding her to him, locking her in his embrace.

And then his arms lessened their grip and his mouth unwillingly left hers.

She felt a moment of inexplicable loss. Then she became aware of what had happened. She took a step back, fighting the shakiness of her legs, and feeling the colour rising to her cheeks.

In response he put his arm firmly round her waist and drew her back to him, saying, 'Come, minx.'

The drunken young bloods gave a cheer and then tumbled down a steep flight of steps, disappearing into a disreputable-looking door.

As soon as they had gone she rounded on him. 'I am no one's minx,' she declared angrily.

'No?' He raised his eyebrows and ran his eyes over her: the rouge and powder, the artfully arranged flaxen hair, the crimson dress.

She flushed as his eyes caressed her soft white neck and drifted down across her low-cut gown. She crossed her arms in front of her, trying to protect herself from his gaze only to see him frown, as though he found it difficult to reconcile the modest gesture with her painted face and provocative gown. And then she saw something else in his face. It was a glimmer of something tugging at his memory; as though he had seen her somewhere before and was trying to remember where, as well as trying to remember who she was.

She felt a coldness invading her. If he knew her . . .

She did not want to follow the thought to its logical conclusion. She took a step to one side and tried to decide which direction to take. Confused by fear she hesitated, not sure which way to go. But his next words galvanized her into action. His perplexed look disappeared and his face cleared.

'Miss Delaware!' he said.

He knew her! And if he knew her, he would surely try and return her to her uncle.

Turning round she fled down the street. As she hurried along she looked anxiously to either side, trying to decide which would be the safest way to go. The main thoroughfares were dangerous, as she had just discovered, and she decided to take a side-alley instead. It was poorly lit and it was unlikely to encourage drunken revellers. Once she had turned into the alley, however, her footsteps began to slow. She went more cautiously, already beginning to think she had made a mistake. She went more slowly still. She could see something at the bottom of the alley. Something or someone. No, a group of someones. Ragged men, seemingly engaged in some sort of transaction. She backed away, but not before they had seen her. She looked at them, mesmerized, for a moment, and then

15

turned and ran back the way she had come.

Footsteps came after her. They were following her! Would she reach the main thoroughfare before she was caught? Yes, she — and then suddenly her heart gave a lurch. Her way out of the alley was blocked. Standing there in the lamplight was the man with the scar, the man who had kissed her.

Good God! How could she have been so blind! She should have recognized him at once! It was Philip Rochdale, the Earl of Pemberton!

She stopped in her tracks. She had a fleeting memory of their introduction at Lady Appleton's ball some months before; then a grunt behind her reminded her of the danger she was in and she ran on. Caught between two dangers she chose to face the one in front of her rather than the worse one behind.

As she came to a stop in front of the earl she saw that a hackney carriage was drawn up at the side of the road. The horse was fretting and stamping its feet.

'Get in!' he said, taking control of the situation. He took hold of her arm and thrust her inside, following her in one lithe movement and closing the door in the face of the three villains who cursed and hammered on the side of the carriage.

The driver gave a shout and the hackney

carriage pulled away.

Madeline watched, terrified, as the three men dwindled into the distance and then turned her attention, scarcely any less terrified, to the man who was sitting across from her in the carriage.

Her first impression was of strength. His face was harsh and hawklike, his sharply defined cheekbones giving definite angles to his face. His jaw was craggy and the scar cut across his cheek like a seam in a rock.

Even so ... even so, although his appearance was hard, her heart was starting to slow of its own accord and her panic was beginning to subside. He might look intimidating, and he might carry with him an aura of power, but somehow it was not the same aura that surrounded her uncle. The earl seemed dangerous, yes, but not wilful or cruel.

She felt some of the tension leave her.

Warily, she began to take him in more closely. He was a little over six feet tall, she guessed, with broad shoulders, appearing broader for the moment because of his many-caped greatcoat. It did not have the profusion of capes that marked the dandy, but nevertheless it marked him out as a man of consequence. Beneath it she glimpsed a coat of blue superfine, a restrained waistcoat and a patch of snowy linen, with cream breeches stretched tight over firm legs. His black leather boots, with their tops turned over, were coated with dust, as befitted a man of action rather than fashion.

As her eyes returned to his face she saw that his amber eyes were looking at her appraisingly.

With what she hoped appeared to be calmness, Madeline returned his gaze. As he made no sudden moves, and as he showed no further inclination to kiss her, she allowed herself to relax a little more, but even so she settled herself right back against the squabs in an effort to stay as far away from him as possible.

She half expected him to say something, but he remained silent. His penetrating eyes watched her thoughtfully.

Was he sure of her indentity, Madeline wondered? Or had it just been a guess? She hoped it was the latter.

'So, Miss Delaware,' he said at last. 'Why don't you tell me what you are doing on the streets without a chaperon, alone and unprotected?'

Hearing him utter her name for a second time, Madeline felt her heart begin to beat more rapidly. She looked about her, feeling her fear beginning to rise again, but there was no way out of the carriage. Giving herself a mental shake, she forced herself to calm down. When she felt in control of herself again she said coolly, 'You are mistaken, sir. I am not Miss Delaware, nor do I know anyone of that name.' If he knew who she was he would undoubtedly return her to her uncle, but if she could just convince him that he was mistaken, that she was what she appeared to be, a woman of dubious morals who happened to bear a passing resemblance to Madeline Delaware, then she might yet be safe. 'I am Miss . . . ' She had been going to say Smith, but it was too obviously contrived. The carriage was at that moment passing a row of shops, and the name of one of them caught her eye. 'Miller.'

He looked at her steadily for a minute. 'Is that so?' he asked with a lift of his eyebrows.

She swallowed, but met his gaze. 'Yes.'

For a moment their eyes locked, and she had the unnerving feeling that he was recalling the rumours that were circulating about Gareth Delaware and his treatment of his niece.

'If you can bring yourself to trust me, Miss Delaware, I may be able to help you,' he said.

Madeline pressed herself back against the squabs. Trust him? A man? Never.

'It was at Lady Appleton's ball that we

were introduced, was it not?' he asked softly.

Her heart jumped. 'You are mistake — '
But suddenly there seemed no use denying it.
He had not only remembered who she was,
he had even remembered where they had
met. Her voice fell. 'I . . . yes, I believe it was.'

Surprisingly, his face softened and he
smiled. But despite this, she still did not trust
him. Because now that he knew who she was,
what was he going to do with the
information? she wondered.

'You said — you said you may be able to
help me?' she asked him cautiously.

The carriage began to slow. She glanced
out of the window and saw they were pulling
up in front of a large town house. It was an
imposing residence, with iron railings separating it from the pavement. A short flight of
steps led up to a magnificent porticoed
entrance.

The carriage stopped. Without answering
her question Lord Pemberton climbed out.
He went round to her side of the carriage and
handed her out. Her skin tingled as he
touched her, and she pulled her hand away,
confused. Why did she tingle when he
touched her? she wondered. And why had she
felt so strange when he had kissed her?

Lord Pemberton gave no indication that he
had noticed anything unusual, however. He

guided her up the steps that led to the front door. Their way was lit by two flambeaux, one on each side of the door.

Madeline hesitated. Should she really go into the house with him? It was dangerous. She turned and looked down the street. Unconsciously she shook her head. Going into the house might be dangerous, but wandering the streets was even more so. And as for going back to her uncle . . .

She took a deep breath, and went into the house.

2

'Why, Lord Pemberton — ' The motherly housekeeper stopped mid-sentence as, coming from the back of the house, she caught sight of Madeline.

'Ah, Mrs Green,' said the earl. 'Miss . . . Miller has met with an unfortunate accident. She was separated from her party on the way to the theatre and was then set upon by a group of footpads, who amused themselves by reducing her to the state you see her in now. Be so good as to show her upstairs, and provide her with the means of washing and a decent gown.' He looked at Madeline judiciously. 'Miss Emma's dresses should fit her well enough, at least for the present,' he said.

'Very good, my lord,' said Mrs Green, rather dubiously, but if she wondered what was the true explanation of Madeline's presence she did not wonder aloud. Lord Pemberton was her master, and it was her job to serve him, not to speculate on the nature of his guests. 'If you'll follow me, miss,' she said to Madeline.

'Go ahead,' said Philip as he saw Madeline

hesitate. 'We'll talk again once you've changed your gown.'

'Oh, I had almost forgotten, my lord,' said Mrs Green, turning round as she began to conduct Madeline up the stairs, 'Mr Fellows is here. Crump has shown him into the library.'

'Mr Fellows?' asked Philip in surprise. 'How long has he been here?'

'Not long, my lord. He arrived barely five minutes ago.'

'Thank you, Mrs Green.'

What brings Jason here? he wondered, as Mrs Green disappeared up the stairs with Madeline in her wake.

At that moment Jason Fellows himself appeared from the back of the house.

He was a good-humoured gentleman with a pleasing countenance, and at this moment his face wore a grin. 'I didn't realize you had company,' he said as he caught sight of Madeline following Mrs Green upstairs. 'Don't worry, I'll show myself out!'

'It isn't what it seems,' said Philip. He removed his greatcoat and steered Jason back towards the library.

'No?' Jason sounded incredulous.

'No.' The two men went through into the library. 'Drink?' Philip asked, as he took the stopper out of a decanter which was placed on a small table by the fireplace.

Jason settled himself down in a wing-backed chair. 'I don't mind if I do.'

Philip poured them both a small whisky and then, flicking the tails of his coat behind him, he sat down opposite Jason, on the other side of the fireplace.

The two men had met at university but on leaving their paths had diverged. Jason now had the soft features and almost boyish manner of a man about town, whilst Philip had the hardened look of a soldier, a man who had spent his adult life on the continent, and most of it on the battlefield. It wasn't just his naturally hawklike features that gave him such a strong presence, nor his lean, firm-muscled body; it was something about his air. There was an alertness about him, a strength and litheness, that Jason did not have.

'So, what brings you here?' asked Philip. He took a drink from his glass and then put it down on the table beside him as he settled himself more comfortably in his chair.

'I was just passing, on my way to the club,' said Jason. 'I thought I'd call in and see how you'd got on with your lawyers.'

Philip shrugged. 'As well as can be expected. Mr Murgo, that is, Mr Murgo the elder, told me exactly what he's been telling me since my father died. That the will is watertight and there's no way round it; that although I inherited the title and the Stonecrop estate when my father died last year, I won't inherit the Rochdale fortune until I've been married for six months.'

'That in itself isn't a problem,' said Jason.

'No,' Philip agreed. 'I fully intend to marry. I may not have had my father's good luck in finding a woman I can love, but at thirty-four I know I must go ahead and marry anyway, to provide an heir for the estate.'

'It's just a shame your father took a dislike to your chosen bride,' said Jason.

Philip nodded. 'It is.'

'Even so,' said Jason, 'I never realized your father's dislike of Letitia went so deep. I didn't think he'd put a clause into his will to try and stop you marrying her, but that's exactly what he's done. Who would have thought he'd make it a condition of his will that you must be married for six months before you can inherit the fortune? And who would have thought he'd stipulate that you can't inherit the fortune even then if you marry Letitia? He's all but made it impossible for you to go through with it. And yet she comes from an old, if untitled, family. And if she doesn't have a fortune, well, the Rochdale fortune is big enough for two.'

Philip was thoughtful. 'I know. But my father took against her. He thought she was selfish, shallow and vain — '

'Which she is,' interrupted Jason.

Philip nodded. 'Which she is. But he knew I needed an heir, and that Letitia was the most suitable bride I could find.'

'He thought you should marry for love, as he did,' said Jason.

'Believe me, nothing would have pleased me better,' said Philip. 'But I was not as lucky as he was. I never fell in love. Still, life goes on. I must marry. My nurseries need filling and I need a countess to run the manor whilst I look after the estate.'

'You're still determined to marry Letitia, then? You don't think, in the light of your father's will, it might be easier to find someone else?'

Philip sighed. 'I've tried. But a year on the marriage mart has convinced me there is no one else I can bring myself to take to wife. If I was a young man, if I was twenty-two or three, then I'd choose a débutante, but I can no longer abide their idle chatter. My years in the army have changed me, hardened me; and if I have to listen to the merits of muslin over sarsenet at the breakfast table for the rest of my life I'll end up in a madhouse!' he added with a wry smile.

'Come now!' said Jason, laughing heartily. 'That's not fair! There must be any number of charming young ladies who can converse intelligently on things beside the latest fashions — art and music, for example.'

Philip groaned. 'Even worse!'

'Well, why not choose a more mature woman, then?' asked Jason.

'More mature?' Philip lifted his eyebrows. 'In my experience ladies get older, but not more mature.'

'You're thinking of Mrs Hardcastle,' smiled Jason. He thought of the wealthy widow who had pursued Philip relentlessly for the last six months, flirting girlishly with him whenever she met him — no mean feat, considering that she was over forty years old!

Philip laughed. 'I must admit she sprang to mind! But seriously, Letitia's the only woman I've ever felt I could marry. She may not be what I'd once hoped for from a wife, but at least she understands the situation and knows the sort of life I am offering her. She is not a young girl who will expect me to fall in love with her and then be hurt when I can't, nor yet an older woman who may not be able to give me an heir. At twenty-seven she is as close as I am going to get to a suitable match: old enough to be realistic about the sort of life she will have with me, young enough to

27

fill the Stonecrop nurseries — and shallow enough to believe that marrying an earl is preferable to marrying for love, if she even has the ability to love, which I very much doubt. Added to that, she's experienced at running a country house and will take a lot of the day-to-day cares off my hands, leaving me free to manage the estate. It isn't what I'd once hoped for from marriage, but under the circumstances . . . ' He shrugged ' . . . it's the best solution.'

'Then all you need is to find a way round your father's will.' Jason took a sip of his drink and then put his glass down on a piecrust table. He pondered the problem of the old earl's will. 'Mr Murgo could offer you no hope, you say? I must admit, it's a thorny problem.'

Philip stretched out his legs and crossed his booted ankles. 'Old Mr Murgo couldn't, no. But the youngest Mr Murgo could.'

'Ah!' Jason nodded in satisfaction. 'So it's good news at last.'

'He didn't want to say so in front of his father and grandfather because his suggestion was — unusual,' said Philip. He gave a wry smile. 'I have a feeling that young Mr Murgo will go far!'

'Unusual?'

'Yes. Unusual — and rather unorthodox.

Which is why he didn't want his father and grandfather to know about it. He followed me out of the office when I was leaving and asked me to meet him later for a mug of ale, in a disreputable tavern in a poor part of town; one he knew his father and grandfather would not visit.'

'You agreed, of course,' said Jason.

'Of course.'

'And what was his idea?' Jason asked.

'His idea was, that if I arrange a temporary marriage with a willing young woman — someone who isn't Letitia — then at the end of the six months I will inherit my fortune.'

'Go on,' said Jason.

'After that, there will be nothing to stop me getting an annulment.'

'Of course!' exclaimed Jason. 'As long as the marriage isn't consummated, then you will be able to have it annulled!'

'And then,' said Philip, 'once it's been annulled, I can compensate my temporary bride for her time and her trouble — she will need some inducement to go along with the idea, after all — and go on to marry Letitia.'

'With the fortune already in your hands! By George!' said Jason, sitting up sharply. 'Young Mr Murgo's right. What a plan! He's a genius.' Then said, with a whistle, 'But it's no wonder he didn't want his father to hear about it.'

Philip nodded. 'No. It is rather a . . . creative . . . solution to the problem.'

'And?' asked Jason. 'Are you going to go through with it?'

'I thought not, to begin with. After all, where would I find a young lady I would want to take to the manor and treat as my wife, even if it was only for six months? The sort of person I would be able to hire to play such a part would not be the sort of person I would want to inflict on my friends and neighbours, even as my temporary countess.'

'Would you have to take her to the manor? Couldn't you stay in London for six months? Or bury yourself at a seaside resort?'

'No. The marriage would have to seem genuine, and as my love for the manor is well known it would not seem convincing if I stayed away for long. And besides, I can't stay away: there is too much that needs my attention in Yorkshire.'

Jason nodded. 'I see what you mean. But couldn't you find some penniless young lady, then? Someone who wouldn't embarrass you, but who would be glad to go through with the subterfuge, in return for a handsome compensation when the six months were over?'

'No young lady would agree to such an arrangement: it would jeopardize her chances of making a permanent marriage. And besides, her family would never let her.'

Jason sighed. 'It's hopeless, then.'

Philip nodded. 'So I thought. I'd already dismissed the idea — when I ran across Miss Delaware.'

'Miss Delaware?' Jason was startled. 'That was Miss Delaware?' he asked incredulously, as he remembered the flash of scarlet satin he had seen following Mrs Green up the stairs.

'It was.' Philip's face became brooding. The sharp lines of his face were deeply etched, and looked even more severe in the candlelight. He took a drink from his glass. 'Tell me,' he went on, 'what do you know about the Delawares?'

Jason shifted uncomfortably. 'Not a lot, really. That is, only what everyone knows.'

'Which is?'

'Which is . . . that Gareth Delaware's a drunken sot who's run through his own fortune, and would have run through his niece's fortune if it hadn't been tied up.'

'And what do you know about his treatment of his niece?' asked Philip.

Jason looked even more uncomfortable. 'That most of the time he keeps her under lock and key. That she's hardly ever seen at parties or concerts or routs, and that even when she *is* seen she's not allowed to speak to anyone, at least not to say more than two or three words, after which her uncle or her chaperon moves her on.'

Philip nodded. That fitted in with his own knowledge, and with what he had seen when he had been introduced to Madeline at Lady Appleton's ball. Strange, the introduction had been several months ago, but its impression had lingered. She had looked very different then, of course. She had been dressed in a simple muslin gown, and her face had been pure and natural, not smeared with gaudy paint, whilst her hair had been demurely arranged. Even so there had been something about her elfin face and haunted eyes that had remained with him. So that almost as soon as he had seen her again, despite her crimson gown and painted face, he had remembered who she was.

But that did not solve the problem of why her uncle had dressed her as a harlot, or why she had been wandering the streets, at night, alone.

'You don't know if he had any plans for her?' asked Philip meditatively.

'Well . . . ' began Jason.

'Yes?'

'I had heard . . . only on the grapevine,

mind . . . that he's heavily in debt again: to Lucius Spalding this time.'

'Spalding? Good God. You don't mean he was planning to marry her to that monster?' demanded Philip.

Jason looked unhappy. 'It's only what I've heard. But it seems likely. Her dowry would cover his gambling debts. Or so the rumour goes. But what's your interest in her?' he asked. 'Besides the fact that you stumbled across her when you'd left young Mr Murgo?' A look of realization began to dawn on his face. 'You don't mean . . . you're not going to ask *her* to be your temporary bride?' asked Jason in surprise.

Philip turned hawklike eyes on his friend. 'I mean *exactly* that.'

'But won't she bore you every bit as much as any other young lady?'

'Undoubtedly,' said Philip. He gave a wry smile. 'But only for six months.'

⋆ ⋆ ⋆

Madeline followed Mrs Green up the stairs.

As she did so she looked about her with interest. The house she now found herself in was the complete opposite of her uncle's. Whereas Gareth's house was dark and dirty, Lord Pemberton's house was light and bright and scrupulously clean — a tribute to Mrs Green, Madeline supposed.

She was rather unsure of Mrs Green. Her experience of life had taught her to mistrust people as a general rule, servants as well as equals. It was Miss Handley, after all, who had been her chief gaoler at her uncle's house. But the housekeeper seemed to have no inclination to watch her or bully her, and simply showed Madeline into one of the guest-rooms.

'I'll have hot water brought up to you directly, miss,' she said. 'If there's anything you want, you have only to ring the bell.' And then she departed, leaving Madeline alone.

The bedroom was very pretty, and could not have been more different from her own dark and sombre bedroom at her uncle's house. Sprigged drapes surrounded the four-poster bed and matching curtains covered the window. An inlaid dressing-table stood against the far wall, and next to it was a rosewood wardrobe. Over in the corner stood a satinwood bookcase and a dainty chest of drawers. A mahogany washstand, complete with ewer and bowl, nestled in the corner. She was at first hesitant about opening the wardrobe, but Mrs Green having told her that the dresses in the guest-room were no longer worn by Miss Emma, who was staying with relatives in Bath, Madeline finally overcame her scruples. She looked through dozens of gowns, marvelling over the pretty yet discreet styles. She finally chose a white muslin with a scoop neckline and little puffed sleeves and laid it on the bed.

As soon as the water arrived, brought up by a neat maid, she washed the powder and paint from her face, feeling much better as soon as she had done so. Then she began to undress.

What help did Lord Pemberton propose to offer her? she wondered, as her thoughts returned to the hawklike man below. She stripped off the crimson dress. Did his sister perhaps need a companion, or . . . she blushed furiously as another, more unwelcome, idea leapt into her mind. There was only one kind of proposal a man would make to a young lady whose reputation was ruined — and she knew that, having left her uncle's protection, her reputation was ruined for ever. How could she have been so blind?

She sank down on the bed feeling suddenly deflated.

But why, then, if that was the answer, had he treated her so respectfully in front of Mrs Green and told her to change out of the crimson gown? She shook her head. It did not seem to make sense. But whatever the reason she knew she would never agree to becoming his mistress, no matter how strangely intoxicating she had found his kiss.

She pushed the thought aside. It troubled her deeply to remember her response to his embrace, and she preferred not to think about it.

She stood up and returned to the task in hand, putting on the white gown. It was a little tight, and a little short, but the muslin was very soft, far softer than the muslins she was used to, and it was very pretty, being trimmed with a satin ribbon beneath the high waist.

With the change of clothes her self-confidence began to return. She sat down on the bed and thought over her difficult situation. With her mind working clearly once again, she decided what she would do. Once she joined Lord Pemberton downstairs she would thank him for rescuing her, and then forestall his plan to make her his mistress by asking him if he knew of any respectable family in need of a governess. If she could only secure herself a position, preferably a long way away from London, then she would be able to support herself respectably. And, if her luck held, she would be able to escape from her uncle completely so that she would never have to see him again.

Noticing that her hair had fallen loose she did her best to repair the damage before plucking up her courage and going downstairs. She hesitated, wondering which way to go, but a light was coming from under one of the doors. She went towards it. Pushing it open, she found herself entering the library.

A warm glow met her eyes. Tall bookcases shone in the candlelight. The gilding on the spines of the books threw out gleams of gold. Dark-green curtains drawn across the windows kept out the night. It was a room to be used, Madeline realized; a room in which the earl could write his letters at the large desk which was set against one wall, or sit reading in one of the wing-backed chairs that flanked the fireplace.

She was pleased to see that he was alone. She had half expected to see Mr Fellows, but it seemed that Lord Pemberton's guest had gone.

Lord Pemberton himself was standing with his foot on the fender, the candlelight playing over his craggy face. She paused for a moment, studying his bronzed skin, his firm chin and his fierce scar. How had he come by it? she wondered. But she had time to wonder about nothing else as he turned at the sound of the door opening.

He took his foot from the fender and was

about to speak when she forestalled him by saying:

'Lord Pemberton. I want to thank you for your kindness in rescuing me from the dangers outside, and to ask if you could help me to secure a position. If you know of any respectable family in need of a governess — '

'Kindness be damned!' he interrupted. She looked startled, and before she could reply he said, 'When you know me better you will realize that I am not in the habit of being kind. I rescued you, as you put it, because I wanted to. And before you talk any more nonsense about becoming a governess, you will do me the courtesy of sitting down and listening to the proposal I have to put to you.'

'That is just it,' said Madeline, 'I can't. I'm not that kind of person.' She straightened her shoulders and lifted her chin. 'I'm grateful for all you've done for me, but I cannot accept *carte blanche*.'

His eyes lit with amusement, and he threw back his head and laughed. '*Carte blanche*! My dear Miss Delaware, that is just as well, as I would not dream of offering it.'

'You wouldn't?' She was bewildered. 'But . . . ' She remembered the feel of his lips on hers and the way his body had pressed close to her own. A strange weakness came over her at the memory, and before her legs could give way she sank into one of the chairs.

'Ah,' he said thoughtfully. 'The kiss. I behaved unforgivably. At the time I thought you were . . . something else . . . and kissing you seemed the simplest way of convincing the drunks you were under my protection and therefore not worth the trouble of molesting. I could have knocked them down, of course, but it seemed preferable to solve the problem without resorting to violence.' He sat down opposite her in the other chair. 'No. My proposition is of a different kind.'

Madeline, recovering a little, was curious to hear what he had to say.

He stretched his legs out in front of him and frowned, as if finding it difficult to know where to begin. 'You know that if your uncle comes here I will have no authority to keep you from him — '

He got no further. Madeline, leaping to her feet, declared, 'I will not go back to him.'

She faced him determinedly, steeling herself for the angry shouts she expected would follow. Whenever she had stood up to her uncle, either shouts or threats had always followed. But to her surprise, none came. Disconcerted, she warily resumed her seat. 'I can't go back,' she said more quietly. 'If you would help me, give me a reference, I could find myself employment — as a governess, perhaps, or a companion. I could go right away from London, somewhere my uncle will never find me. I know it is a lot to ask but — '

'That won't be necessary,' he said. 'There is another way.' He paused, as though choosing his words carefully. 'Miss Delaware, I am faced with a dilemma. If you agree to help me it will solve your problem as well as my own.'

She was interested now. 'Go on.'

'Very well. My dilemma concerns the subject of my inheritance.' He paused, frowned, and then continued. 'My father died just over a year ago but, because of one of the clauses in his will, I did not immediately inherit the Rochdale fortune. I will not be able to inherit it until I have been married for six months. That in itself does not present a problem. I fully intend to marry, but unfortunately my father did not like my choice of bride. So that, if I marry Letitia, I will lose the fortune for ever.'

'I'm . . . sorry,' she said.

He smiled, a warm smile. It brought his face to life and she found it strangely attractive.

'However, there is a solution to the problem,' he said. 'If I arrange a temporary marriage with another young lady — any young lady, so long as she is not Letitia

— and take her home to my Yorkshire estate, I can claim my fortune once I have been married for six months. I can then have the marriage annulled and I can go on to marry Miss Bligh with the fortune already in my hands.'

'Ah! I see.' Madeline was beginning to understand the nature of his proposal. 'And you want me to be that other young lady?'

'I do.'

'But how will that solve *my* dilemma?' she asked. She did not like the idea of a sham marriage but in her desperate situation she was forced to consider it.

'Because once you are my wife you will be able to escape from your uncle. As a married woman, he will have no more power over you,' he said.

'But you will.' She jumped up and paced the room. 'No,' she said, shaking her head. 'No. I cannot do it.'

'I would have power over you as your husband, it is true,' he said, finding himself wondering why she should think of marriage in terms of power. It was not a normal reaction, particularly in one so young, and despite himself he was intrigued. However, Miss Delaware's views on marriage were not his concern. It would not do for him to become sidetracked; he must stick to the

41

matter in hand. 'However, it would only be for a short time,' he went on. 'Once the marriage is annulled, no one will be able to have any power over you ever again. If you agree to my proposal I will make you a handsome settlement when the annulment takes place. You will have a home of your own, and an annuity which will bring in enough money for you to live on comfortably for the rest of your life.' He saw that she looked close to exhaustion. He stood up. 'You don't have to decide now,' he said. 'Why not think it over and give me your answer in the morning?'

'It's no good,' she said with a sigh. She shook her head. 'Even if I could bring myself to agree, my uncle would never give his consent. He has . . . other plans for me.'

'Your uncle has no control over my life. I would not ask his consent.'

'But I am under age.' Her shoulders dropped. 'My birthday may be only a week away, but it might as well be five years away if my uncle finds me. And once he reads the banns he will be sure to do so.'

'Then we will not publish any banns. We will marry by special licence. It has been done before, and will be done again. Young ladies don't always marry with their guardians' approval. You simply ran away before

42

you knew you were to be married, instead of afterwards.'

There was a laughing glint in his eye as he said it, and Madeline realized that he was teasing her. It had lightened the atmosphere and to her surprise Madeline felt the corners of her mouth tugging themselves into a smile. She had had so little to smile about of late that she had almost forgotten what it felt like.

Even so . . .

Even so, the earl was a man, and she knew from bitter experience that men were not to be trusted.

'I can't,' she said, shaking her head. Once again she waited anxiously for an exclamation of impatience, expecting him to be angry or jeering because she did not fall in with his plans. But again, to her surprise, neither anger nor jeers came.

Somehow, she found it unsettling. She had always known how her uncle would react, even if she had been afraid of him, but with the earl she was off balance, never knowing what to expect.

He put his finger under her chin and tilted her face towards his. 'You are tired,' he said. 'You will find your bed has been made up. Go and get some rest.'

She looked up at him uncertainly. Consideration and gentleness were not things she was used to, and for a moment she allowed herself to wonder what it would be like to be the earl's wife.

But then she bid him goodnight. Because there was also a hardness and a frisson of danger about the earl, and she could not marry him, no matter how desperate her situation — or how short-lived the marriage would be.

3

Once back in her room, Madeline sat down in front of the inlaid dressing-table and stared sightlessly into the looking-glass. She did not ring for a maid to help her undress. She preferred, for the moment, to be by herself. Because the Earl's marriage proposal had stirred up painful memories, memories buried deep in the past . . .

How old had she been when she had first realized how dreadful her parents' marriage had been? she wondered. She could not have been more than five or six years old. She could still remember the occasion clearly. It had been on a hot summer night when she had wandered down from the nursery, unable to sleep. As she had approached her mother's room she had heard the sound of shouting and had stopped, afraid to go any further. She had put her eye to the crack in the door and had seen her mother sitting on the bed, weeping. Standing over her mother she had seen her father. He had been shouting at her mother. Cruel words. Uncalled for. *Stupid . . . worthless . . .* the tirade had gone on. And then other memories. Memories of her father belittling her mother before the servants and then laughing at her mother's distress; her father making jibes at her mother when the vicar called, leaving the vicar embarrassed and her mother crushed and humiliated; her father laughing at her mother for her thinness and paleness, making her thinner and paler with every word he said. And her mother, when Madeline discovered her one day weeping brokenly, saying to her in an impassioned voice, 'Never trust a man, Madeline. It only leads to despair. And never, ever marry. Marriage is a terrible trap from which there is no escape.'

Madeline recalled her thoughts to the present. With trembling fingers she began to unpin her hair. Her father and her uncle, both bullies . . . Her mother had been right to warn her against men.

And against marriage.

No matter how appealing the idea of having her own home and an annuity was, she could not accept the earl's proposal. Because, curious as a part of her was to know what it would be like to be the earl's wife, a stronger and more frightened part recalled the cruelties her father had inflicted on her mother, and her mother's tearful despair.

She shivered and pushed away the memory of her mother's sufferings. But she did not push away her mother's tragic warning. She could not marry the earl. But she was still grateful to him for having given her somewhere safe to stay, and if she could only persuade him to give her a reference so that she would be able to find a post as a companion or governess and support herself, then she would have nothing more to wish for.

* * *

A governess, she thought the next morning as she swung her legs over the edge of the bed.

It was a bright and beautiful morning, and sunlight was streaming through a crack in the curtains. What a difference between this room and her dingy room in her uncle's house! she thought. The pretty sprigged drapes at the window glowed in the bright light, and the polished furniture shone.

She went over to the window and lifted the curtain, looking down into the neat and orderly garden.

Yes, a governess, she thought, dropping the curtain and going over to the washstand, where the porcelain jug had already been filled.

If she became a companion then she would be condemned to a life of servitude, but if she became a governess then in time she might be able to open her own small school and achieve a measure of independence.

She washed and dressed, dispensing with a corset as she could not manage the laces by herself, and then went downstairs.

Breakfast had been laid in the dining-room, and Madeline helped herself to a plate of ham and eggs. She was surprised to find that she had such a healthy appetite. In her uncle's house it had been all she could do to push a morsel of food past her lips, but here, with the burden of fear lifted from her, she enjoyed her meal. She saw only one servant during all that time: Crump, the butler, who brought her a cup of chocolate, and who told her that the earl had gone out on business but would be back before lunch.

Once Madeline had finished her breakfast she knew exactly what she wanted to do. She had seen a large collection of novels in the bedroom, displayed in a pretty break-fronted bookcase, and she longed to look through it. She had noticed a number of books by famous authors, amongst them Maria Edgeworth, Mrs Radcliffe and Jane Porter, and she was looking forward to browsing through this unexpected treasure. Novels had been forbidden in her father's house, but her mother had occasionally managed to acquire one and she

48

and Madeline had read them together.

Running her fingers along the spines, Madeline smiled as she came across *Evelina* by Fanny Burney. It had been her mother's favourite book. They had both of them delighted in Evelina's adventures as she had moved from the country and discovered the joys of London life — until her father had found the novel. She shuddered, and her finger moved on. *A Sicilian Romance, Castle Rackrent, Octavia* — all the best novels by the best authors were there. At last she selected Anna Maria Porter's *The Hungarian Brothers* and, tempted by the summer sunshine, took it out into the garden.

A riot of colour met her eyes. Emerald green lawns, lovingly tended, were crossed by gravel paths which snaked through the beautiful garden. Large flower-beds were filled with gay blooms, in striking contrast to the rank and overgrown patch of land behind her uncle's house. The roses in particular, just beginning to unfurl, made a lovely display. She stopped to smell them, breathing in the heady scent, feeling as though, after long months and years of merely existing, she was finally coming back to life.

Then, seeing a stone seat set at an angle to catch the morning sun, she walked over to it and settled herself comfortably. The stone was already warm and she stretched herself luxuriously before opening her book and beginning to read.

★ ★ ★

'Ah! Pemberton! There you are. Good of you to come.'

Philip shook hands with the seasoned man who had stood up to address him. They had met by design in a quiet corner of White's, in St James's Street, Philip's London club.

'Your message sounded urgent,' said Philip. 'I thought it best that we should meet straight away.'

Callaghan nodded, and the two men sat down in a couple of deeply buttoned leather armchairs. 'Perhaps not urgent, but important. Oh, yes. And something you will want to know.' He opened an enamelled snuffbox and offered Philip a pinch. Philip refused and he shut the box with a snap. 'I won't waste your time, Pemberton. I know you're a busy man, so I'll come straight to the point. Saunders was a friend of yours, was he not?'

Philip's attention sharpened at the sound of the familiar name. 'He was. And still is.'

Callaghan nodded thoughtfully. 'Seen anything of him lately?'

Philip sat back and surveyed the man in

front of him. To outward appearances Callaghan was an ordinary man. More weather-beaten than most, perhaps, but nothing more. And yet Philip knew him to be a spy.

The war in Europe was dragging on. Although Napoleon had suffered a number of defeats in recent years he had still not been stopped. He seemed determined to prolong the war for as long as possible, knowing that if he sued for peace his own power would be lost. The activity of spies, therefore — men who regularly risked their lives to find out where he would strike next, or what his numbers were — was vital if the war was to be brought to a speedy end. They lived in a dark and shadowy world; a world of intrigue, deceit and double agents, of sudden danger and silent death. And in this dark and shadowy world moved men like Callaghan. And men like Jack Saunders; the man who, three years before, had saved Philip's life — a debt that, if the opportunity ever presented itself, Philip meant to repay.

But for now he could do nothing to help Callaghan. 'No. Not since I left Spain. Why? Has something happened to him?'

'We're not sure. We lost touch with him some weeks ago.'

Philip's voice was emotionless: years of

fighting on the continent had taught him that tragedy was inevitable in such a conflict. 'Which means that he is injured, captured or dead.'

Callaghan's face remained bland. 'Not necessarily.'

Philip's gaze sharpened. Callaghan wasn't some green boy who clung on to hope for no good reason. He was an experienced campaigner. A cautious experienced campaigner. 'And what is that supposed to mean?'

Callaghan did not immediately reply. His face became blander by the second. 'It means that Saunders was engaged on . . . delicate work. There may be reasons why he has not been in touch.'

Philip's eyes narrowed. He knew Callaghan would not say anything more definite, but that did not stop him from speculating as to what the delicate work could be. Going under cover, perhaps? Infiltrating Napoleon's staff? — made easier by the fact that Napoleon was running desperately short of men and needed all the help he could find. Or was the delicate work something of a different kind? Was it a matter of trying to weed out the double agents who played both sides off against each other, in the certainty of coming out on top no matter which side won? Yes, that was possible.

'Why would he contact me?' Philip asked.

'He knows you. He trusts you. If something's wrong he may not want to go through the regular channels . . . or he may not be able to. We have to investigate every possibility. He's not been . . . '

He stopped as a waiter approached their corner and asked if he could get either of the men anything. They answered in the negative, and did not speak again until he had left.

'He's not been in touch with you?' asked Callaghan, finishing his question.

'No,' said Philip. He said no more.

Callaghan nodded thoughtfully. 'You'll let us know if you hear from him?' he asked.

Philip looked at him appraisingly. He was a good judge of character — his years in the army had honed his original instincts in that direction — and he felt that Callaghan was a man to be trusted. But even so he would only reveal any contact if Jack himself wanted him to do so.

Callaghan smiled, as if reading his thoughts. 'That is, if Saunders has no objections?'

Philip gave a curt nod.

'Good.' Callaghan stood up. Then, for the benefit of anyone who might be listening, he said in a hearty voice as the two men left the club, 'Good to see you again, Pemberton! Next time we mustn't leave it so long!'

The two men parted, Philip frowning as he thought over what Callaghan had said.

He did not like it. No, he did not like it one bit. Jack wasn't the kind to lose touch with his superior officers unless it was unavoidable, no matter how delicate his mission might be; and if it was unavoidable, that meant trouble.

Still, Jack was capable of handling trouble. And right now, thought Philip, as an image of Madeline rose before his eyes, he had his own concerns.

★ ★ ★

The Hungarian Brothers was turning out to be even more interesting than *Evelina*. Madeline, absorbed in her book, was enjoying herself. The sun was warm and a pleasant buzzing of the bees, interspersed with the occasional cooing of the doves, created an idyllic backdrop to the romance. Lord Pemberton's house was only a short distance away from her uncle's house in Grosvenor Square, but it seemed to be in a different world. It was calm and peaceful; all the things her uncle's — and her father's — house had never been. She was just about to turn the page when she was disturbed by a sound coming from the direction of the house and, looking up, was amazed to see Jenny hurrying towards her through the garden.

'Jenny! What are you doing here?' she asked, laying down her book and going to greet her maid. 'How did you find me?'

'Oh, miss,' gasped Jenny, who had obviously been running hard, and who was clutching her side where a sharp pain had formed with the effort. 'I've come to warn you, miss. Your uncle's found out where you are and he's coming to get you. He's already on his way.'

Madeline looked at her uncomprehendingly. 'No, Jenny, you must be mistaken. He can't have found me.' But even as she said it she began to realize it must be true. Jenny had found her, and if her maid could find her then so could her uncle.

Icy fingers clutched at her heart.

'He's had the servants looking for you all night,' went on Jenny. Her breathing was still laboured, but she was determined to speak. 'He sent everyone out. He was in such a taking. They've been combing the streets, but they couldn't find you. You don't know how glad I was to think you'd got away! But someone saw you, miss. Some drunk. He saw you getting into a hackney carriage with the Earl of Pemberton. And now your uncle's on his way here to fetch you back again. But don't you let him take you, miss. Don't you ever go back to him, or he'll make you pay for having run away. There's no telling what he might do if he gets you in his clutches again.'

Madeline began to pace, too distracted to ask how Jenny had found the house and gained entrance, or even to wonder at it. She could only think of one thing. She was not going back with her uncle. If he found her in the garden she would be an easy target. She must go back inside.

'Quickly,' she said to Jenny. 'We must go inside. I'll speak to Crump and give him instructions not to admit . . . '

But it was too late. A violent altercation was coming from the direction of the house, and a minute later her uncle appeared, Crump following and still protesting that Mr Delaware could not come in.

Madeline looked wildly around but the garden was bounded by a high wall and there was no escape.

'There you are!' seethed her uncle. His face was contorted with anger and he was almost purple with rage. He strode towards her, ignoring Crump and Jenny. 'By God! You're a cunning little bitch! Thought you'd set up for yourself, did you?'

Madeline shrank back, afraid of him and

humiliated by his words. As if she would . . . would . . . she couldn't bear to think what he was implying.

But her uncle did not stop. He advanced on her menacingly and as she turned to run he caught her by the wrist, his fingers like a vice and his nails biting into her flesh. 'Oh, no, miss. You're not going anywhere. Your dowry's going to pay my gambling debts. You're coming back with me.' His face suddenly broke into a warped smile, and Madeline found it almost worse than his rage. 'I never would have thought you had it in you, Maddy. A chip off the old block after all.' He gave a leer. 'And you've not done bad for yourself. I told you that dress would work wonders. Look what it's done for you. Set you up as Pemberton's mistress. Pemberton! A bloody earl! If I didn't need your dowry to pay off Lucius Spalding, by God I'd applaud!'

As he spoke, Madeline, trying to twist her wrist out of his grip, suddenly saw Philip striding across the garden. She closed her eyes, racked with humiliation as she realized that he must have overheard. She made a renewed effort to wrench herself free whilst Philip, just returned from his club, strode towards them across the garden, his face like thunder.

That is how he must look on the battlefield, she thought as she saw him. His long, lean body was rippling with sinew and muscle and a wave of power seemed to emanate from him, flooding the air with danger.

'Delaware!' His voice cut the air like a whip. 'Get your hands off my wife!'

Gareth sneered, although he took an involuntary step backwards all the same. 'She's coming with — what did you say?' he asked as the earl's words sunk in. 'Your *wife?*' And then he quickly recovered. 'Oh, no, Pemberton, you don't play that one with me. You have no claim on her. She is my ward. My *twenty-year-old* ward. She's under age, Pemberton; under *my* care and protection. You'll have to find yourself another bit of muslin.' His face took on its customary leer. 'Although this one'll take some beating, I agree.'

'That is the second time you have insulted Lady Pemberton,' said the earl, the wave of danger intensifying. 'Do so again and I will call you out.'

Gareth dropped Madeline's wrist and a look of fear crossed his face. The earl had fought on the Peninsula. His reputation was formidable. 'Now, look here, Pemberton,' he said shakily. 'You can't do this. She isn't your wife. You know she isn't.' His tone was almost pleading.

'The countess and I were married by special licence this morning. Which means that she is no longer under your 'care and protection', Delaware. She is under mine.'

'You . . . You . . . ' spat Gareth, words failing him as his rage momentarily overcame his fear. Then, 'You'll never get her dowry,' he said, holding his ground and squaring up to the earl; only to quail a moment later before the latter's aura of power.

'I don't want it.' The earl spoke contemptuously.

'You don't want ten thousand pounds'?' asked Gareth incredulously.

'It would barely cover the countess's pin money. You may keep her dowry. Provided,' he said, his voice becoming like polished steel, 'that neither I nor the countess ever see or hear from you again. Is that understood?'

'I . . . ' Gareth's eyes were calculating. He felt ill used, but he was loath to make a fuss. With Madeline's dowry he could pay off his debts, and what use was she to him anyway? Without her dowry she was no use at all. Quite the opposite, in fact. She was a hindrance. True, her dowry was tied up so that he could not touch it, but if her husband did not want the money why, then, should it not come to him? The earl had only to claim it and then pay him off, and if he played his cards right he might even be able to make some capital out of the situation. Once it became known that his niece had married Pemberton he would get an extension on his credit, if he was lucky. Besides, though he had blustered, he knew that there was little he could do about it if Madeline was already married. Such marriages — marriages made without the agreement of the young lady's guardian — were not unheard of, and making a fuss might do more harm than good; especially as the earl had all the power of rank on his side.

Gareth appeared to consider. 'I don't like it,' he said grudgingly at last. 'You have played me a dirty trick. But — yes. It seems I have no choice. I agree.'

'A wise move,' said Philip. 'And now, you have polluted my house for long enough. Crump will show you out.'

Gareth looked as though he might choose to stay and create further trouble, but one look at Philip's implacable face decided him. He gave a curt nod and followed Crump back into the house.

'Are you all right?' asked Philip, striding over to Madeline.

But she ignored his question. 'You had no

right to say that,' she declared.

He stopped in his tracks.

'I have not agreed to be your wife,' she said.

A part of her realized that his deception had saved her from her uncle, but an older and deeper part of her was afraid. Only last night he had told her that she had a choice in the matter of her marriage; he had made her think she could agree to his proposal or reject it as she chose. But by telling her uncle they were married he had taken that choice away from her.

'I have just — ' he began.

'Taken my choices away from me.'

'I have done nothing of the kind,' he said. 'If I had not told your uncle we were married he would have had every right to take you back — though how he found you in the first place, God knows,' he added.

'As to that, the answer is simple,' said Madeline. Her anger was beginning to fade. 'A drunk saw me getting into the carriage with you, and told my uncle's servants what he had seen. My uncle sent them out looking for me,' she explained. She shook her head and shivered, suddenly feeling cold. 'I should have known he would not let me go so easily.'

'He told you this?' asked Philip curiously.

'No.' Turning to Jenny, Madeline said, 'It

was Jenny who told me. She came to warn me that my uncle had discovered my whereabouts.'

Noticing Jenny for the first time, Philip said, 'That explains it.' He became thoughtful. 'Well, it is a good thing Jenny is here,' he said at last. 'You are in need of a maid.' He turned to Jenny. 'I take it you do not wish to go back to Mr Delaware?'

'Oo, no, sir,' said Jenny, agog with all she had just witnessed.

'Then that is settled. I have some business to attend to,' he said to Madeline, 'but we will speak again after lunch. There is still much we have to discuss.'

★ ★ ★

'Only think, miss,' said Jenny as she dressed Madeline's hair some half an hour later. She had followed Madeline up to her bedroom and helped her to dress properly, lacing her corsets for her, before repairing the ravages done to her hair. 'Now you're the Countess of Pemberton I'll have to start calling you 'my lady' instead of 'miss'.' She had not been fully able to follow the conversation in the garden, but she had heard enough to believe that the earl and Madeline were married.

'No, Jenny.' Madeline watched her maid's

deft fingers arrange her hair. 'I am not the Countess of Pemberton.'

'But the earl said . . . '

'I know what the earl said. But I am still not the Countess of Pemberton. It is true that the earl has asked me to be his wife — he needs to arrange a temporary marriage in order to claim his inheritance, and he has asked me to play the part of his wife. But he told my uncle that we were already married so that Gareth would not take me back to Grosvenor Square.'

'Oh, I see,' said Jenny. 'So,' she went on, 'when is the wedding to be?'

'There is no wedding,' said Madeline.

'But you just said . . . '

'I said he *asked* me,' said Madeline. 'But I have refused.'

'Refused!' Jenny's busy fingers fell idle in amazement.

'Of course I have refused,' said Madeline. 'After what I have seen . . . '

'But the earl isn't like your uncle, my la — miss,' said Jenny, shaking her head as she continued with her work. 'He's a different sort of man is the earl. They all say so, all his servants, and servants always know. I've been friendly with Hinch, the parlour-maid, for a long while now — we met by accident on our afternoon off some months ago, and struck up a friendship, and that's how I got in, miss; as soon as I heard where you were I came at once, and Hinch, she let me in at the back — and she's always spoken well of her master. Treats his servants well, he does, and — '

'Servants are one thing,' interrupted Madeline, not wishing to talk about it. 'Even my uncle treated his servants well for the most part. But — '

'Not just his servants,' said Jenny resolutely, arranging Madeline's hair into a chignon and pushing in pins to hold it in place. 'His friends . . . and his women friends, too.' She should not be talking about the earl's 'women friends' to Madeline, but Madeline had seen and heard a lot of unsuitable things whilst in her uncle's house, and besides, showing the earl's character as it did, it was something Madeline needed to know. 'Treats them — not like ladies, but like human beings, miss — courteous, like, and friendly, not showing them up and humiliating them, like your uncle. And not just his friends and his women friends. He treats his sister well too.'

Madeline shook her head. 'Even so, it is too great a risk. As my husband he will have too much power over me. I have asked him to provide me with a reference and I intend to try and find a position as a governess instead.'

Jenny said nothing, but her silence spoke volumes.

'As a governess I will be respectable,' said Madeline. 'I will be able to earn my keep. And I will be safe from my uncle.' As she spoke she realized that she was trying to convince herself of the wisdom of her choice, rather than Jenny. 'And perhaps, in time, I may be able to open a small school of my own.'

'Just as you say, miss.' Jenny's tone showed that she didn't like the idea. She had been with Madeline since Madeline's childhood, and was very protective of her mistress.

'You don't approve?'

'It's not for me to say, miss,' said Jenny woodenly.

'I *can't* accept the earl's offer,' said Madeline. She stood up and began to walk round the room. 'I have no guarantee he will honour his side of the bargain. He says he will provide me with a house and an annuity when the marriage is annulled, but I have only his word for it. Once I am in Yorkshire I will be alone, with no one to turn to — trapped again.'

'And once you're a governess?' asked Jenny obstinately.

Madeline sighed. 'I know. It is fraught with

problems too. The master of the house may be another man such as my uncle. And the earl is at least honourable.'

'And you spent last night under his roof without coming to any harm,' Jenny reminded her.

Madeline nodded. She had been half afraid to go to sleep the night before, being under the same roof as a strange gentleman and knowing how so-called gentlemen could behave, but she had passed the night in safety and comfort.

'And he would have a good reason for treating you right,' said Jenny. 'If he didn't, you could run away and he wouldn't get his fortune. He needs to present himself, with his wife, to the lawyers at the end of the six months, I think you said?'

'He does.'

'So it stands to reason he'd treat you well,' said Jenny.

Madeline crossed the room again, more slowly this time. Her brow was furrowed in concentration. If the earl did as he said then her problems were over. If not . . .

She sighed. Marriage to the earl was risky, but it was also her best option. He was unlikely to treat her badly because he needed her. Even if he did not, as he had promised, provide her with a house and purchase her an annuity, then at the end of the six months she would be no worse off than she was now. And it was not true that she would be alone. She would have Jenny with her, she reasoned; which she would not have if she took a position as a governess. But still, could she do it? Could she take such a chance?

Her mother's warning came back to her. *Marriage is a trap*, her mother had said. But this marriage would not be a trap. This marriage had its end built into its beginning.

Resolutely Madeline made her decision. She would accept the earl's offer. However risky that offer might turn out to be.

★ ★ ★

Madeline went downstairs. Having made her decision she acted on it straight away, and found Lord Pemberton in his study. He was writing at his desk as she entered, but as soon as he looked up and saw her he threw down his quill and stood up.

She straightened her shoulders and smoothed her skirt, then she said, 'Lord Pemberton. I have come to ask you if I can change my mind.'

'About?' he asked.

'About becoming your wife.'

'Does this mean that you accept my

proposal?' he asked.

'I — yes. It does.'

He smiled, then sat on the edge of his desk and folded his arms across his chest. He looked younger, friendlier. He stretched his long, firm legs out in front of him. 'May I ask what made you change your mind?'

'It was Jenny.'

'Jenny?' he asked in surprise.

'Yes. She told me . . . she has friends among your servants . . . and they all speak well of you, she says.'

He gave a shout of laughter.

'What's so funny?' she asked.

'This,' he said. 'This situation. When you came in I was writing you a reference so that you could take up a post as a governess — and at the same time Jenny was giving a reference for me!'

Madeline's face broke into a smile. 'A commoner must seek a reference from an earl, but an earl, being already at the top of the tree, must go full circle and get one from his servants!' she giggled. The absurdity of the situation overcame her, and she collapsed into laughter. As she did so she realized that she had not laughed for years.

But she quickly recovered herself. She knew very little about the man in front of her and although she had agreed to enter into a sham of a marriage with him she knew she must not let down her defences.

He, too, had sobered. 'We will marry as soon as you are twenty-one,' he said, becoming businesslike. 'I don't think your uncle is likely to make any further difficulties, but as your birthday is only a week away I suggest we wait until you are of age. It will make it far more difficult for him to cause trouble if he changes his mind.'

Madeline nodded in agreement. What the earl said made sense.

But there were other things she needed to know. 'What will happen afterwards? When the marriage is annulled?'

'Why, I will claim my fortune and go on to marry Letitia. And then — '

'Is the fortune really so important to you?' she asked. Despite the fact that she had agreed to the six-month marriage she thought it strange that Philip, in love with Letitia — or so she believed — would arrange a sham marriage, even to claim his fortune. And stranger still that Letitia, being in love with Philip, did not object.

'Yes. It is. My estate is badly run down. My father loved it, but as he got older he neglected it, particularly after my mother died. And as I was away fighting Napoleon I could not take a hand. Without the fortune I can't maintain the estate, let alone improve it. I can't repair the tenants' housing, and I can't introduce new measures on the home farm to make it more successful — in fact, I can't do any of the things I need and want to do. And once I have claimed the fortune,' he said, 'I will provide you with a handsome annuity, and a choice of houses to live in. I own many properties in and around York, and you can choose which one you please. Or, if you prefer, I will buy you a respectable house in the country.'

'And you are sure that you will be granted an annulment?' she asked.

'I am. As long as the marriage is not consummated, there will be no difficulty in having it annulled. The only problem you may not have thought of is that if you want to marry again your bridegroom may wonder why your first marriage was annulled.'

'That won't be a problem,' said Madeline definitely. 'I have no intention of marrying again.'

'You are very young to be so sure,' he said, looking at her curiously. Once again Miss Delaware had intrigued him, and that was not normally something ladies did, young or old.

'Nevertheless I *am* sure.'

'Is it because of your uncle's behaviour?' he asked.

'That and . . . other things.'

He looked at her searchingly for a minute but then, to her relief, he allowed the subject to drop.

'As soon as we are married we will set out for Yorkshire,' he said. 'The journey is a long one, but we will take our time. You have been out of London before, of course?'

'When I was a child I lived in Hampshire,' she said. 'But I have never been to the north.'

'Then you should prepare yourself for a surprise. The landscape is harder, but grander too. I think you will like it. But now to more important matters. By the time we arrive in Yorkshire you will need some suitable clothes.'

He scrutinized her closely, and Madeline realized how little she must look like a countess.

'My sister's clothes are all very well for here,' he said, 'and will have to do for the journey, but as soon as you arrive at Stonecrop you will need something more suitable to wear. My sister uses a very skilled modiste here in London, a Madame Rouen, who can take your measurements and help you choose some fabrics before sending the details to her cousin. Her cousin is a York modiste,' he explained, 'and by the time we reach Yorkshire you will find a number of dresses ready and waiting for you.'

'You seem to have thought of everything,' said Madeline. There was a tension in her voice, as though she wondered whether the earl meant to control her life.

'Not everything. You will be free to organize your own time in Yorkshire, I promise you.' He reached out his hand and pushed a stray tendril of hair behind her ear. 'I will be busy with the estate, and it will be up to you to do as much or as little as you wish. You don't need to be apprehensive about the coming months, Madeline. You have nothing to fear.'

Except the way I feel every time you touch me, thought Madeline with a strange shiver.

But she kept that thought to herself.

4

The day of the wedding was cold and wet. The summer sunshine had given way to a spell of unsettled weather. It matched Madeline's unsettled feelings — relief at having escaped from her uncle on the one hand, and wariness about the coming six months on the other. Because despite Jenny's arguments in his favour, and despite the things she herself had seen, she still knew very little about the earl and she was determined to be on her guard.

As she walked down the aisle on Jason Fellows' arm she saw Philip waiting at the altar for her. He was looking imposing in a blue tail-coat, pale-blue waistcoat and cream breeches. His dark hair was brushed à la Brutus, and his amber eyes were glowing brightly in the red and gold light that fell through the stained glass windows.

There were few other people at the ceremony. Young Mr Murgo was there, standing beside Philip, together with a clergyman, whilst sitting in the pews at the left-hand side of the church were a well-dressed gentleman, an extremely elegant young lady and an elderly woman of mousy appearance who was evidently her companion.

The young woman — young still, though she was a good five or six years older than Madeline — was expensively dressed and had an air of consequence about her, as though she knew her own place in the world, and as though that place was an exalted one. Her hair was a rich chestnut colour, and she was very beautiful. She gave an arch smile as Madeline walked past her, but Madeline had no time to wonder who she might be as another few steps took her to the altar, where Philip was waiting for her.

The ceremony began. It was a brief, formal affair. There were no hymns or readings, just an agreement by Madeline and Philip to take each other as husband and wife, a joining of hands and a pronouncement by the clergyman that they were man and wife.

And then it was over. For good or ill, Madeline was no longer a spinster. She was Philip's wife.

A brief picture of her mother flashed before her eyes, but fortunately she had no time to think about her mother's unhappy fate as the elegant young woman immediately rose in a cloud of expensive scent and went over to Philip, taking his arm with a proprietorial air.

'Philip.' She turned her face up to his in the most charming manner. 'I am so glad you are married,' she purred.

'Madeline, may I present Miss Bligh?' asked Philip, turning to Madeline.

Of course! That was who the elegant young woman must be. Miss Bligh, Philip's intended bride.

She was undeniably beautiful, and extremely elegant. She carried herself like a countess already, her tall, willowy figure showing off her expensive and fashionable clothes to great advantage. Even so, Madeline could not help being surprised at Philip's choice. For all her beauty and elegance, there was a hardness in Letitia's eyes that spoke of a selfish nature, and a curl of her mouth that suggested disdain. However, Philip's choice of a bride was not her concern, and so she reminded herself.

'What a clever idea to hold the wedding here,' said Letitia, looking round the small church with a patronizing air. 'It would have been dreadful to have held it in town, with a horde of people gawping at you. It is so cosy here. So . . . obscure.'

She gave a smug smile, as though contrasting the small church with the splendid church in which she herself intended to be married.

'But Philip, do tell me when you are leaving for Yorkshire,' she went on, turning her back on Madeline and effectively cutting her out of the conversation.

Leaving Letitia and Philip to their discussion, Madeline began walking towards the door of the church, meaning to see if the rain had stopped, but before she had gone half way the gentleman who had been sitting with Letitia accosted her and swept her a low bow.

'Lord Hadley, Countess,' he said, turning mocking eyes towards her. 'But let us not stand on ceremony. You must call me Robert. I'm Letitia's cousin.'

'Lord Hadley,' said Madeline with a slight inclination of her head.

'Ah! Madeline! You cut me to the quick! Will you not call me Robert? But I see that you won't. A pity, as we are . . . connected . . . you might say. You are Philip's first wife, and my cousin is his second! Although we must not speak of that here,' he said in an exaggerated whisper. 'One never knows who might be listening.' He made a pantomime of looking round.

There was something jeering in his manner and Madeline did not respond to his sally.

He gave her an arch look. 'You don't find it a subject for mirth, Countess? But I do. I find it delicious. A sham marriage to claim an

76

inheritance. What a stroke of genius. Philip is a lucky man. He not only gets Letitia, he gets the fortune as well.' He looked at Madeline thoughtfully, and a gleam of malice entered his eye. 'But what, my dear Madeline, is in it for you?'

'That is between the earl and myself,' said Madeline shortly. She had no intention of telling Lord Hadley about her private affairs, nor indeed of continuing the conversation.

But Lord Hadley was not to be so easily put off. 'It's very good of you to go through with it,' he said, refusing to let the subject drop. 'Very noble and disinterested. On the surface, at least. But what, I wonder, lies underneath?'

Madeline had had enough of such an unpleasant conversation and decided to put an end to it. 'Good day, Lord Hadley,' she said coldly, then turned on her heel.

'A word of warning,' he said, moving to block her path. There was a note of menace in his voice. 'If you're thinking of double-crossing Letitia, then you'd better think again.'

'Let me pass,' said Madeline.

But Lord Hadley did not stand aside, and when Madeline took a step to go round him he countered her move. 'Why would a sensible woman — and I'm sure you're a sensible woman, my dear Madeline — why would a sensible woman marry an earl and then let him go, I ask myself? The answer is, she wouldn't. She would marry him, yes, but give him up — give up all that power? Give up all that wealth? No, a sensible woman would hang on to him. And how would she do that? The answer is obvious. By tempting him to consummate the marriage.' His eyes became hard. 'It's a good plan, Madeline, but one I suggest you abandon.' There was a threat in his voice now. 'Letitia doesn't like to be crossed, and believe me, she isn't someone you'd want to have as an enemy.' And then he smiled once again. 'Remember that, won't you? It is good advice.'

'Ready to go?' came Philip's voice behind them.

'Ah! Philip. I was just congratulating your beautiful countess on her marriage,' said Lord Hadley smoothly.

'I'm sure you were,' said Philip levelly, but the look he gave Lord Hadley was a searching one. 'However, it is time for us to leave. Madeline?'

He gave his arm to Madeline and together they went out to the waiting carriage, leaving Letitia and Lord Hadley behind.

Letitia wore a decidedly pleased expression as her eyes followed them out of the door.

She looked like a cat who had eaten the cream.

'I hope you know what you're doing,' remarked Lord Hadley, looking after Madeline. 'You're playing a dangerous game, my dear.'

'By allowing Philip to marry? I don't think so. Little Miss Delaware's pretty enough in an unassuming sort of way, but she's no great beauty, and even if she was, young girls fresh from the schoolroom have never been to Philip's taste. Besides, I had to let him marry. Without the temporary marriage he wouldn't be able to claim his fortune, and I can't wait for ever whilst his lawyers try to find another way round his father's will.'

'No, that would never do,' said Lord Hadley sardonically. 'Philip must have his fortune. God forbid that you should marry him without it.'

'What would be the point of that? Really, Robert, sometimes you are just too stupid. If I am to become a leading member of the *ton*, if I am to have influence and power, then I must have the fortune. Rising to the top requires money; money for clothes and jewels, money for renovating the London house and the Yorkshire estate — what a pity it's so far away from London,' she added vexedly, before continuing, 'however, it will have to do — money for hosting glittering parties, money for entertaining royalty; if I am to have money for all these things then I must have the fortune.'

'*You* must?' he asked mockingly.

'Philip must,' she shrugged. 'It amounts to the same thing.'

'And does he know just how mercenary you are, my dear?'

She raised her finely drawn eyebrows. 'Philip has few illusions. He knows the fortune is important to me. Even so, a sensible woman keeps the less attractive sides of her personality to herself.'

Lord Hadley laughed. 'I have to admire you, Letitia. You may be cold and calculating but you know what you want, and you know how to get it.'

Letitia's beautiful face hardened. 'I do. And what I want most of all is to be the Countess of Pemberton.'

'You're magnificent,' said Lord Hadley admiringly. 'Does nothing frighten you?'

'Nothing,' she said, 'except poverty and obscurity. Which is why I have taken a few precautions, in case little Miss Delaware and Philip should get too close to each other in the coming months. I have made sure that one of the servants at the manor is loyal to me. It was easy enough — a little matter of a down payment, and the promise that he will become the new butler once I am safely installed at the manor. Then if Madeline and Philip get too close I will hear about it, and I will know what to do. *I* am going to be the Countess of Pemberton, Robert, and nothing — and no one — is going to stand in my way.'

* * *

The sound of the dinner gong reverberated through Philip's London house. With one last tweak of her gown Madeline went downstairs. She would be pleased when her own gowns were finished; Emma's gowns were a little too tight for her curvaceous figure, and she would be more comfortable in clothes that were a proper fit.

The earl was waiting for her outside the dining-room and they went in together, sitting in state, one at each end of the long table. To her surprise, Madeline found that she was hungry: it had been an eventful day.

'Did you enjoy your afternoon?' asked the earl, as one of the footmen served him with a bowl of green-pea soup.

'Thank you, yes.'

Madeline had spent the afternoon at the modiste's, choosing a few final items for her wardrobe. The experience had been as pleasurable as her previous visits over the last week, and she had not been able to help making a comparison between her own and her mother's lives. Her mother had never been allowed to choose anything for herself, whereas Madeline had been free to choose her entire wardrobe, selecting the styles and colours that suited her and that she would find enjoyable to wear.

As they ate their meal, with servants serving each course — a baked turbot with truffles, stewed venison and finally a pyramid of sweetmeats — they talked of Madame Rouen's ideas, and then of the topics of the day, but when the servants had been dismissed Madeline found her thoughts drifting back to the wedding ceremony and the time she had spent in church.

Philip looked at her curiously and then, throwing down his napkin, said, 'Something is troubling you.'

'No. You are mistaken,' she remarked uncomfortably.

He leaned back in his chair, his amber eyes penetrating. 'Don't try and fool me, Madeline. It doesn't work. Something is definitely troubling you. Are you regretting it?' he asked. 'Going through with the marriage?'

She shook her head. 'No.'

He nodded thoughtfully. Then suddenly he

asked, 'What did you think of Letitia?'

The question took Madeline completely by surprise. 'She is . . . very beautiful. And very elegant.'

'Yes. She is. Letitia is the most polished woman I have ever met.'

Does he really think so? Madeline wondered with an unaccountable sinking feeling. Before reminding herself that it was no business of hers what he thought.

'She seemed to know all about it,' Madeline said with assumed nonchalance. 'Our . . . arrangement.'

He nodded. 'She does.'

'And does she not object? To your marrying someone else?' Madeline asked, trying to make her voice light and unconcerned.

'Would *you* object?' he asked. 'If the positions were reversed.'

'Most definitely,' she said. The words came out too quickly, and she flushed.

He looked at her searchingly, as if trying to read her thoughts. Then he said, 'Letitia doesn't want to be poor any more than I do. She has plans for the future, as I have, and those plans require my fortune.' He pushed back his chair and stood up.

'I see.'

'But it seems wrong to you, our six-month

marriage?' he asked, looking down at her with a frown.

'It isn't for me to judge. After all, without the six-month marriage, I would not have been able to escape from my uncle.'

'Yes, you would,' he surprised her by saying, and the intensity of his gaze unsettled her. 'You would have become a governess, or a companion, and although your life may have been hard you would still have escaped from your uncle. In fact, I am beginning to wonder if I was wrong to talk you into this,' he said, as though speaking to himself.

'No.' She shook her head forcefully, pushing back her own chair. 'You suggested the idea, but I was the one who agreed to it.'

A faint smile appeared at the corner of his mouth, his expression one of respect. She gave a shiver. There was something about the sight of his face softening that made her melt inside. What it was she did not know; unless it was the contrast between his craggy features and the full lines of his mouth.

His eyes lingered on her and she swallowed, feeling a sudden tension in the room.

'Come,' he said. He seemed to feel it too, and to make a deliberate attempt to dispel it. 'Let us retire to the drawing-room.'

She nodded. 'Very well, my lord.'

'Philip,' he said, dropping his arm and taking her hands instead. He turned to face her. 'My name is Philip.'

She pulled her hands out of his own. She didn't know how it was, but somehow his touch made her tremble. He seemed to feel it, too, and to her relief he did not try to reclaim her hands.

'I can't call you that,' she said.

'You're my wife, Madeline. You can't go on calling me 'my lord'.' There was a hint of amusement in his voice, but she found the idea of calling him Philip too disturbingly intimate.

But then she gave herself a mental shake. She was being foolish. Of course she must call him Philip. He was right. She was now his wife. 'Very well . . . Philip.'

He put his finger under her chin and turned her face towards him.

'There. That wasn't so difficult, was it?'

'No.' But standing there, as his strong fingers traced the line of her cheek, was. It sent ripples of awareness through her, and she gave an involuntary shiver.

Why was she feeling this way? she wondered. She knew what men were: brutal, controlling and savage.

Yes. Brutal, controlling and savage.

She took a step back. 'If you will excuse

me,' she said, taking control of herself, 'I am feeling rather tired. I will bid you goodnight.'

★   ★   ★

Once more in her room, Madeline was relieved to find that Jenny did not notice how quiet she was. Instead, her maid was full of chatter, a chatter she was happy to encourage, because whilst Jenny talked she did not have to examine her own confused feelings. Brutal, controlling and savage; yes, that was what men were really like, and if Philip did not seem to be the same it was because he needed her in order to claim his inheritance. No man would be brutal towards someone who was to help him inherit a fortune which was, by Philip's own admission, immense. It was after men had gained the promised fortune — their wife's dowry, in most cases — that the problems really began. But fortunately for her, once Philip had claimed his fortune the marriage would be over, instead of just beginning, and she would no longer be his wife. There would be no risk of brutality; no risk of the fate that had befallen her mother becoming her own, just a house of her own and an annuity so that she could live out the rest of her life in freedom and independence.

'Hinch has been telling me all about Yorkshire,' Jenny said, as she helped Madeline out of her gown. 'And, mercy me! It sounds almost like another country. The Yorkshire folk — that's what they call people up there in Yorkshire, my lady, *folk* — the Yorkshire folk speak an odd sort of language called dialect. Now what do you think of that?'

'I don't know, to be sure,' said Madeline, forcing herself to concentrate on Jenny's lively chatter.

'They say some funny things,' went on Jenny. ''Put wood in 'tole'. That's one of the things they say. And what d'you suppose they mean by that?'

'I don't know.'

'Neither did I, my lady, but it means, would you believe it, 'shut the door'!'

'Shut the door?' asked Madeline in surprise. 'Jenny, you must have got it wrong.'

'No, my lady.' Jenny shook her head firmly. ''Shut the door'. Put the wood in the hole, you see, my lady, that's what it means, and if you think about it, it makes sense. When you put the wood in the hole that's what you're doing, isn't it? You're shutting the door!'

Madeline laughed until the tears ran down her cheeks. 'Oh, Jenny, it can't be true!'

'It is, my lady,' said Jenny determinedly. 'As God is my witness — and oh! my lady, up there they swear God's a Yorkshireman, would you believe? — but as God is my witness I'm telling you the truth, just as Hinch told it to me. And she's not one for funning, my lady, isn't Hinch.'

'But how will we understand anything they say?' asked Madeline, her gale of laughter gradually subsiding. She wiped a tear of laughter from her cheek.

'Well, to be fair, my lady, it's only the country folk who talk like that. So Hinch says anyway. The ladies and gentleman, they talk like you and me. Though they say their words differently,' she added judiciously as she unpinned Madeline's hair. 'They say bath, my lady,' she said, making the a hard and short, 'instead of 'baaarth'.' She drew out the sound to make the difference clear.

'We will have our work cut out for us. Still, whatever happens in Yorkshire, it seems we will not be bored.'

Jenny unlaced Madeline's corsets for her and, removing her chemise and drawers Madeline pulled her night-gown over her head.

'No, my lady,' Jenny agreed as she folded Madeline's things.

Despite Jenny's lively chatter, Madeline still felt restless as she climbed into bed. Try as she might, she could not ignore the fact that this was her wedding-night. What would it have been like, she wondered, if she and Philip had been really married?

Determinedly she pushed the thought away. She picked up her book and, by the light of the candle, began to read, until at last Miss Porter's tale about the Hungarian brothers sent her off to sleep.

5

Madeline awoke with a start. The bedroom was still dark. What time is it? she wondered.

The moon was up. She could see its light through a crack in the curtains. But what was it that had awoken her?

She had a vague feeling that it had been a loud crash.

This was not what she had expected of her first night as Philip's wife.

She sat up in bed and listened, wondering if burglars had broken into the house. There had been a spate of robberies recently, and her uncle had taken extra precautions against the malcontents who roamed the streets of the capital. Had one such broken into the earl's house?

Slipping a shawl around her shoulders Madeline left her room and, by the light of the moon, made her way cautiously along the landing.

She heard the sound of voices coming from below.

Taking her courage in both hands she crept downstairs, meaning to find out what was happening before rousing the house; she did not want to raise the alarm, only to find that the crash had been caused by a drunken footman, or a maid who could not sleep.

As she reached the bottom of the stairs and followed the muted sound of voices she saw that there was light spilling out of Philip's study. She went forward then stopped just outside the door, looking in.

The first thing she saw was Crump over by the window, picking up the pieces of a smashed vase.

So that was what had made the noise.

Madeline hesitated. Now that she knew the cause of the crash had been nothing more serious than a broken vase, should she go in, or should she go back to bed?

Then she saw Philip. He was looking strong and virile. He had evidently just been getting undressed when he had heard the noise, and his clothes were in disarray. He wore no coat or waistcoat, but was in shirt and breeches, the clothes defining the muscular contours of his lean body. His shirt was open, revealing a glimpse of powerful chest.

Madeline looked away in confusion. She had seen a number of men in a state of partial undress in her uncle's house, during their many drinking sessions, but they had filled her with nothing but disgust. Why, then, did the sight of Philip provoke such a startlingly different reaction?

At that moment Philip looked up and saw her. An intense light lit his eyes, and an unreadable expression crossed his face. Was he angry? Madeline wondered. Pleased? Or simply surprised to see her there?

He crossed the room in two strides until he was standing just in front of her.

'What happened?' she asked, fighting down the tingling sensations that threatened to engulf her. There was something about Philip that set her skin on fire, but what it was she dared not think. Instead, she turned her attention back to the room. Something had happened, and she knew she would not sleep until she had discovered what it was.

'There is nothing to worry about,' he said, lifting his hands as though he was about to put them on her shoulders, and then, thinking better of it, dropping them again. 'Go back to bed.'

'Was it burglars?' she asked.

He hesitated. As he did so his eyes fell to her night-gown and she felt a sudden tension in him. 'You should not be down here like that,' he said.

'I did not have time to dress,' she returned, pulling her shawl more tightly about her.

He turned away abruptly, so that she would not see the effect she was having on him.

'How did they get in?' she asked.

'Through the window,' he remarked.

Madeline looked over to the windows, expecting to see that one of them was broken, but they were all intact. 'It isn't broken,' she said, puzzled.

Philip hesitated, as though wondering how much to tell her. Then, seeming to decide to tell her something, at least, he sat on the edge of the desk and faced her. 'They were professionals,' he said. 'They prised the window open until the gap was wide enough for them to slip a wire inside and undo the catch.'

'Then, if they hadn't broken the vase, we would not have known they were here,' said Madeline with a shudder.

Philip nodded. 'That was careless. But they were in a hurry.'

'Have they taken anything of value?' she asked.

'That's just it, my lady,' said Crump, entering the conversation for the first time, 'they don't seem to have taken anything at all.' He looked from Madeline to Philip, perplexed.

'Then we are lucky,' said Philip smoothly. But something in his tone of voice made Madeline aware that there was more to this situation than met the eye. 'Crump and I will see to the clearing up. I suggest, Countess, that you go back to bed.'

'I — ' She was about to protest when she realized that he would not, or could not, say any more for the present; and besides, she was growing cold. 'Very well.' Now that she knew the house was not in any danger she felt her presence was no longer necessary. And she would find it easier to be away from Philip's unsettling presence. It was bad enough in the daytime: by night it was even worse.

Philip, watching her go, felt a sense of relief when she had departed. He sat for some minutes, watching the space where she had been, and wondering why he had reacted so strongly to the sight of her in her night-gown. True, he had reacted strongly to the sight of her in the crimson gown she had been wearing when he had first seen her, but then he had mistaken her for a harlot. But now, knowing that she was as innocent as she was chaste, the reaction still remained; and he realized that for one uncontrolled moment he had almost given in to an impulse to steer her back to her bedroom and reveal to her the passions of a normal wedding night.

Why was he reacting like this? he asked himself with a frown. It was not as though he was an untried boy, losing control of himself because a passably pretty woman — a beautiful woman — a deeply beautiful woman, he thought, his eyes tracing the delicate curve of her cheek in his memory, the smooth arch of her neck, the tantalizing swell of her breast and the rounded curve of her hips — happened by chance to enter his life. He was a thirty-four-year-old man, with all the experiences that thirteen years of maturity entailed. But still, she stirred him.

No matter what his feelings were, however, he could not give in to them. Because in order to have the marriage annulled he had to make sure it was not consummated.

He was beginning to realize just how difficult that was going to be.

* * *

It was at breakfast the following morning that Madeline discovered more about the night's events. Philip had just finished eating when she entered the dining-room, and as she sat down to hot rolls and a cup of chocolate he said, 'I am sorry you were disturbed last night. I hope you managed to sleep when you went back to bed?'

'Yes. Thank you.'

'Good.' He looked at her searchingly.

'Madeline.' He paused, as if not quite sure how to continue. 'For reasons I cannot disclose I would rather you did not mention the break-in to anyone. Apart from ourselves, the only other person who knows about it is Crump, and he will not speak of the matter without my leave.'

'Very well,' conceded Madeline, 'if it's important.'

'It is.'

'But won't the servants wonder how the vase was broken?' she asked.

'If they do, Crump will say he broke it himself by accident.'

Madeline frowned as an unwelcome idea occurred to her.

'What is it?' he asked, seeing she had laid down her knife. 'You are not eating.'

'I just wondered . . . Are you in any kind of danger?' she asked.

'Of course not.'

'If you are in danger I have a right to know,' she continued, not convinced by his denial, and concerned for his safety.

'No. You don't,' he remarked. Whatever the cause of the break-in, he did not want Madeline involved. He pushed his chair back from the table and stood up, bringing all further discussion to an end. 'Finish your breakfast. We will be leaving as soon as the coach is loaded. I intend to set out within the hour.'

★　★　★

The Rochdale coach was large and spacious and Madeline travelled inside it for the first part of their journey north. The day was bright and the weather was warm — a perfect day for travelling.

Once they had left the city behind, however, Madeline took to horseback. She would have felt conspicuous riding through heavily populated areas without a proper riding-habit, Emma's wardrobe being unable to furnish her with such an item, but once away from the crowds her unsuitable clothing no longer troubled her. She enjoyed riding the white mare Philip had brought along for the purpose. Their pace was slow and steady, and they covered not more than three or four miles an hour.

'What do you think of the countryside so far?' asked Philip as his horse fell into step beside hers.

Madeline cast her eyes over the verdant hedgerows and rolling fields, then let them linger on the colourful wildflowers that grew in profusion by the side of the road.

'I think it's beautiful,' she said.

'It is. Beautiful. And worth protecting.' His voice was unusually soft.

Sensing that he was in a rare mood to talk, Madeline made the most of the opportunity, wanting to know more about the man she was to spend the next six months with.

'You're thinking of the war?' she asked.

'Yes.'

'Did the break-in last night have anything to do with your time in the army?' she asked. There must have been more to it than met the eye, she realized, or else Philip would not have asked her not to mention it to anyone, and throughout the day the incident had never been far from her mind.

She thought for a moment that he would not answer her question and half expected him to ride away, but although she could tell by his frown that he did not like it, nevertheless he answered:

'It may have done.'

'And that is why you didn't want me to mention it?'

'In wartime, loose talk can cost lives,' he remarked.

Madeline nodded. 'I understand.'

They rode on for a while in silence. Then Madeline asked 'How did . . . ?' She stopped, aware that she might be intruding into his private life, a life she knew almost nothing

98

about. But she wanted to know.

'Go on.'

'I was just wondering. How did you get your scar?'

She had an urge to reach out her hand and trail her finger along the strangely attractive seam.

What would it feel like? she wondered. Would it be rough or smooth? She shivered as she imagined the feel of it beneath her fingers.

But she should not be thinking such things. They were dangerous.

With difficulty, she turned her attention back to the present.

'Ah. The scar.' He said nothing, and she thought she had offended him by mentioning it. But after a few minutes he said, 'It was out on the Peninsula. We had made camp and settled down for the night, when we were caught unawares. Sentries had been posted, but they were quickly dispatched before they could raise the alarm. I woke to find a Frenchman not ten feet away from me. I drew my sword, but before I could get to my feet he lunged at me.'

Madeline shuddered.

'I was lucky to survive,' Philip went on. 'I would *not* have survived if my friend had not knocked the Frenchman's sword aside. The deflection was just enough to make sure I ended up with a scar, instead of ending up dead.'

'Mr Fellows must be a brave man,' said Madeline, thinking of the friend who had been present at Philip's house on the night she had met him, and who had been present at their wedding.

Philip shook his head. 'Not Jason. He's a good friend, but he was never in the army. No, this was someone else.'

He almost told her about Jack, but the news from Callaghan had been worrying and he did not want to talk about his friend until he knew he was safe.

'Were you sorry to leave the Continent?' she asked. It seemed a strange question, and yet she sensed that although he had not enjoyed the war, he had wanted to fight to protect his country, and with it his beloved estate.

'In a way. I felt I was leaving with the job half done. But once my father died I knew my place was here. We'll defeat Boney in time. It's more a question of when than if.'

'Do you really believe that?' She had heard many conflicting opinions about the war — her uncle's cronies had loved to talk about it, although she suspected they had known little about it — and she was interested to know the opinion of someone who had first-hand knowledge.

'Yes, I do,' said Philip. 'He's had a lot of luck, but luck doesn't last for ever. Not even with a man such as Bonaparte. He's made a lot of mistakes recently. He tried to conquer Russia and he failed. He set out with over six hundred thousand men, but came back with only twenty thousand. And it's not only men he lost. He lost wagons and horses as well — things he will find it difficult to replace.'

Madeline tried to imagine what it must be like on the battlefield. 'It must change you. Fighting in a war like that,' she said softly.

He turned melting eyes towards her. 'For one so young, Madeline, you have a surprising understanding of life.'

There was a moment's breathless silence as his eyes ran over her face. 'My life has been — unusual.' She paused, then asked a question that had troubled her for some time, in an attempt to turn the conversation back into safer channels. 'When you found my uncle at your house would you really have called him out?'

Being with Philip was proving to be more difficult than she had anticipated and she made an effort to keep her mind on the conversation.

He didn't answer her question, but instead

asked one of his own, as if he wanted to learn more about her.

'Would you have minded?'

She nodded. 'Yes. I would.'

'After all he has done to you?' His voice was surprisingly tender, and the look he gave her made her tremble unaccountably.

She gulped, in an effort to swallow down the new and disturbing sensations that were assailing her.

'I don't approve of bloodshed,' she said. 'In war I know it is necessary. But in ordinary life . . .'

'It may surprise you, but neither do I. My years in the army changed me, but they did not turn me into a monster.' He turned to look at her fully, and his face softened. His eyes ran over her fair hair and her elfin face and came to rest on her beautifully shaped mouth. 'In answer to your question, no, I would not have called your uncle out. He is older than I am, and out of condition. It would not have been a duel, it would have been slaughter.'

'And if he had chosen pistols instead of swords?'

Philip gave a wry smile. 'Rumour has it that your uncle is a dreadful shot.' He became more serious. 'I have seen enough of fighting, Madeline, and don't want to see it again. I threatened your uncle because I knew he'd back down.'

They rode on in silence, each in their own thoughts. Madeline was asking herself how it was that she was enjoying Philip's company so much and Philip, to his surprise, found himself thinking of Letitia.

What was it that made him think of her now? he wondered as he rode along beside Madeline. Was it because she was the complete opposite of Madeline, and because he found that knowledge disquieting? Letitia would have loved him to have fought a duel over her — the fact that a man had died for her would have appealed to her vanity. She wouldn't have been horrified at the violence, she would have gloried in it. But then Letitia was a vain woman who cared only for herself, whereas Madeline had a depth and maturity to her character that he had never met with in a woman before. Her sufferings at the hands of her uncle, although they had brought her a lot of anguish, had also brought her wisdom and understanding; things that age alone could not give.

He turned to look at her. She was lovely in profile. Almost as lovely as in full face. But still, she was very young, and young ladies one step removed from the schoolroom had never been his style.

'We will be stopping soon for the night,' he said, looking ahead as though he recognized the road.

'Have you chosen an inn?' asked Madeline.

'Yes, the Nag's Head,' said Philip. 'It isn't far now.'

As he spoke the outriders began to pick up speed, the six horsemen riding on ahead to arrange suitable rooms for the earl and countess. It was one of their many useful purposes, Madeline realized: by the time she and Philip arrived at the inn everything would be ready for them.

The outriders were soon lost to view and the coach rumbled on with Madeline and Philip riding beside it. They rounded a bend . . . and saw three masked horsemen on the road ahead. Immediately Philip swung his horse round, but another three masked horsemen appeared from the woods at the side of the road and closed in behind the coach.

Madeline felt her heart leap into her throat. There were masked men both in front of them and behind them. They were trapped.

'Do nothing,' said Philip in an undertone to Madeline, his eyes narrowing into slits as he watched the three men in front of them ride slowly towards the coach.

'Are they highwaymen?' asked Madeline in

an aside, patting the neck of her nervous mare in an effort to steady the animal.

Philip's voice was grim. 'Highwaymen don't travel in packs.'

There was time for nothing more. One of the masked men had ridden forward even further than his fellows, and whilst they covered Madeline, Philip and the coachmen, together with various servants who formed part of the entourage, with their pistols, the foremost man dismounted. With his pistol at the ready he threw open the door of the coach. He swung round, pointing the pistol directly into the coach, then, seeing it empty, climbed in for a more thorough search.

From her vantage point on horseback, Madeline watched him as he searched under the seats and then looked on in horror as he took out a knife and began slashing the squabs.

'What's he doing?' she whispered to Philip.

'I don't know,' he replied in an undertone. 'But I believe he's looking for something. Or someone,' he added as if to himself.

The masked man then proceeded to tap the floor, roof and sides of the coach, sticking his knife in at various points as if to satisfy himself that nothing was being hidden there.

Then, apparently convinced, he climbed out of the carriage. He cocked his gun and pointed it at Philip.

Philip did not flinch.

The two men faced each other for a fraction of a second. Then the masked man lowered his gun, turned on his heel and sprang back on to his horse.

As quickly as they had come, the masked men melted away.

'What was the meaning of that?' asked Madeline in concern.

'I don't know,' said Philip, his face grim. 'But I intend to find out.'

The outriders were at that moment returning — having arranged for the night's accommodation, they had realized the coach was slow in arriving and had turned back to see what was causing the delay — and Philip called out to the two foremost.

'You, and you. Come with me. The rest of you see the coach safely to the inn.' He turned to Madeline. 'I have to leave you now, but I'll meet you at the Nag's Head.'

And swinging his horse he set off in the direction the masked men had taken, followed by the two outriders.

Madeline, shaken by the incident but curious as to why the coach had been searched, was left with no alternative but to do as he said.

The inn was soon reached. Pondering over

the day's events, Madeline went up to her room. She washed and changed, freshening herself after the journey, and then waited for Philip to return.

* * *

It was late when Philip finally arrived at the inn.

'What have you discovered?' asked Madeline as he walked into their private sitting-room. He looked tired, she thought. She longed to stroke the hair back from his face, but knew she could not do it.

He threw down his gloves. 'Nothing,' he said, sounding dissatisfied.

'But you know why we were stopped.' It was a statement and not a question.

'Madeline,' he said. 'There are things in my life that are better hidden. At least for now.'

'When you asked me not to mention the break-in to anyone, I agreed, but I will no longer be kept in the dark,' she said, gently but firmly. 'I asked for an explanation then but you refused to give me one. Now, however, the danger has increased and I will go no further until I know what this is all about.'

'You will do as you are bid,' he said wearily. Being cold and tired, he was in no mood to explain the situation to Madeline, especially as he did not fully understand it himself. 'You are my wife — '

'And I must therefore do as you say?' she asked.

'Yes,' he said abruptly.

'But I will not,' she informed him, thinking how wise she had been to keep up her guard. For all the rapport they shared, Philip was still a man, and she was glad she had not trusted him. She did not intend to let him dictate to her: she had seen all too clearly where that would lead. Instead she knew she must stand up to him.

'We made a bargain,' he said, his brows drawing together. 'You agreed to play the part of my wife — '

'But I did not agree to risk my life,' she returned. 'I need to know why the coach was stopped.'

'The more you know, the more risk there is,' he said. 'The less you know, the safer you are.'

'I will be the judge of that,' she returned.

'Madeline — ' he began.

But she would not let him finish. 'I will go no further until I know what kind of danger I am in,' she said firmly. 'And why.'

He looked at her penetratingly for a moment, as though to gauge how determined she was, then gave a curt nod. 'Very well.'

There was nothing conciliatory in his tone, and Madeline felt a moment of doubt. What if she *was* safer not knowing what dangers threatened? What if knowing put her at greater risk? Philip had spent many years in the army. The war was still raging just across the Channel. There were things in his life, perhaps, it was better not to know.

But it was too late to change her mind now.

'Do you remember when I told you about my scar?' he asked.

Madeline nodded. 'You told me that without the help of one of your friends, you would not just have been scarred, you would have been dead.'

'That's right. The friend I told you about did not leave the army when I did. Instead he remained. But not as part of the regular forces. He became a spy.'

'A spy?' asked Madeline. It seemed she had stumbled into something much more serious than she had realized.

'We need spies,' said Philip curtly. He had misunderstood her tone of voice and thought she was condemning the work of spies; that, like many other people, she felt it was underhand and devious, not fit work for a gentleman. 'They do a dangerous and thankless job. They discover vital information.

Without them we wouldn't know when Napoleon was going to be making his next move, and where he was going to strike.'

'And your friend is involved in this?' asked Madeline.

'It's possible.' Philip's voice was still hard.

'Then the masked men were looking for him,' said Madeline. She was beginning to understand the situation. For a moment a part of her wished that she had not demanded to be told, so that she could still think she was involved in nothing more than the commonplace dangers of burglars or highwaymen.

But that was ridiculous, she told herself, straightening her shoulders. It was better by far to know the truth. Because if the last week was anything to go by, then the coming months might be full of such incidents, and the more she knew about the cause of the incidents the better.

'Possibly,' said Philip. 'Either that, or they were looking for information. Perhaps secret information that he has uncovered, information that would be dangerous to the French.'

'And the break-in? The people who were responsible for that were also looking for your friend? Or his information?'

'It certainly seems that way.'

'And what did you discover now? When

you followed the masked men?' asked Madeline.

'Nothing.'

Madeline heard the frustration in his voice.

'They had too much of a head start,' Philip went on. 'We followed them for some way, but our horses were tired from the day's journey and theirs were fresh. In the end we lost them. And now, Countess, you know everything I know,' he said curtly.

He moved to leave the room, but even so she needed to know more. As he walked over to the door she said, 'Do you think they will trouble us again?'

'I don't know,' he said, turning. 'But probably not. I have, however, taken precautions. I have instructed the outriders they are not to leave the coach for any reason — if their constant presence means they can no longer ride ahead to pay the tolls, so that we are delayed at the toll gates, and that they can no longer organize our rooms in advance so that we have to wait whilst our rooms are prepared at the various inns along the way then so be it. The coach will not be unprotected again.'

He spoke coldly, stiffly, and Madeline realized that the rapport which had grown up between them on the earlier part of the journey had been destroyed.

For some reason she could not begin to fathom, she realized she cared about its loss.

But it was too late now to do anything about it. Philip had already walked out of the room, closing the door behind him.

Madeline walked over to the window. But it was not the pleasant landscape, basking in the last rays of daylight, that she saw. Instead it was the incidents that had recently beset them. When she had married Philip she had known the undertaking was perilous, but she was beginning to realize there were other perils connected with the venture, perils that had nothing to do with the marriage; perils she could not possibly have foreseen.

★ ★ ★

Philip pulled off his boots with a feeling of profound dissatisfaction. Once back in his room he could no longer hide from the fact that the day had been full of frustrations. Not only had his attempts to discover who had attacked the coach been unsuccessful, his subsequent conversation with Madeline had proved disastrous. And all because he had been trying to protect her.

Where had it come from, this need to protect her? he wondered. Why had he not just told her the truth about the danger she was in and left her to grapple with the information as best she could? Why had he wanted to shield her? She was nothing to him. She was not someone he cared about, he told himself. Of course not. She was simply the means by which he intended to claim his inheritance.

And yet, was that not the problem? That Madeline wasn't *simply* anything. Nothing about her was simple. And nothing about his reaction to her was simple either. First of all he had found himself unaccountably — and damned inconveniently — attracted to her, and now he found himself wanting to protect her as well. It didn't make sense. She was nothing but a chit of a girl, and should not in any way be influencing his life.

So how was it that, alone in his room, he could think about nothing else?

★   ★   ★

The following morning they set out again. They now went more swiftly than before. Unwilling to linger on the road, Philip set a brisk pace and Madeline took to travelling for most of the day in the coach, despite its despoiled squabs. Although she enjoyed riding she found the new pace demanding, and she preferred to travel for at least a part of the day in the coach.

By the afternoon, however, she had grown tired of being confined and she took to horseback once more. She did not ride by Philip's side as she had done the previous day, but rode next to the carriage whilst he rode on ahead. The hostility of the previous evening had not evaporated, and they had spoken scarcely two words to each other since setting out.

Before long, however, he fell back to ride alongside her. As he did so, the carriage turned off the road and went through a set of imposing gates.

'We will not be staying at an inn tonight,' he informed her. 'We will be staying with Lady Weatherby, my great-aunt.'

'But we can't just call in on her unexpectedly,' protested Madeline.

'I sent a messenger to her with a letter a few days ago. She will be expecting us,' he said. Although he was riding beside her his manner had not relented, and his voice was still cold.

'And . . . does she know? About our arrangement?' asked Madeline hesitantly.

'Oh, yes,' said Philip with a slight nod. 'She knows. It would have been pointless to try to deceive her. Aunt Honoria may be old but she's shrewd. She would have seen through

114

any subterfuge at once.'

Madeline was in a way relieved. She knew that at some point she would have to be able to convince Philip's friends and relatives that she was his true wife, but she was glad that she did not have to do so just yet, because she was not sure if she could play the part convincingly. In company, perhaps, at a large dinner party, or at a ball, where she would not have to speak to any one person for long, but not in such an intimate situation.

Philip paused, then said, 'It will be as well for you to be on your guard, even so. Aunt Honoria can be — unpredictable. She has strange fads and fancies.' There was a slight thawing of his manner as he spoke, as though their enforced conversation had done something, at least, to heal the breach between them.

'Is it wise, then, to stay with her?' asked Madeline, pleased he had unbent a little.

'Yes.' He spoke definitely. 'It is better to meet her at a time and place of my choosing rather than her own. Old though she is, she would have travelled to Stonecrop to meet you if I had not arranged for us to visit her on the journey north. And if she is planning any mischief I would rather she did it here.'

'What kind of mischief is she likely to plan?' asked Madeline a shade anxiously.

'It's impossible to say.' Philip gave a wry smile. 'She has an . . . original . . . mind.'

'Is she likely to expose the masquerade?' asked Madeline.

'I don't know. I don't think so. She doesn't like Letitia any more than my father did, and I wouldn't put it past her to create difficulties of some kind, but as to actually exposing the nature of our marriage, I think it unlikely. Even so, it is better to be prepared for anything. With Aunt Honoria it's never possible to be sure.'

The coach turned off the main road.

After passing between two stone pillars it wound its way up a long gravel drive. The drive was dark, being overhung by gnarled old trees and sombre bushes, but finally the coach emerged into sunshine once more. And there ahead of them was a glorious, sprawling pile.

'The house is Jacobean,' said Philip. 'It has been in the family for over two hundred years.'

Sunlight sparkled on the windows which Madeline could see were made up of tiny diamond-shaped pieces of glass. The house itself was a muted red, which stood out from the surrounding green gardens, creating an imposing spectacle.

There was a hustle and bustle as the

servants sprang into action. Madeline and Philip dismounted, and then approached the imposing entrance.

Once inside, Madeline felt apprehensive. The entrance hall was like a cavern, with stone-flagged floors and a huge stone fireplace. Suits of armour stood to either side of the fireplace, and above it hung a collection of antiquated weapons; maces, morning stars and fearsome-looking double-handed swords.

An ancient butler led them upstairs. Heavily carved tables and ponderous chairs in solid oak were pushed back against the walls. But when they reached the dowager's sitting-room at the back of the house Madeline received a pleasant surprise. Although the furniture was still the heavy oak furniture she had seen elsewhere, there was an air of cheerfulness about the room. Fresh flowers stood on the mantelpiece and tables; the upholstery was of bright, instead of dull, red and gold; and the sunshine spilling into the room through the diamond-paned windows made it a welcoming place.

Sitting on a chair so large and heavily carved it could almost be called a throne, was Philip's aunt.

Madeline saw at once where Philip's hawklike air came from. Lady Weatherby's eyes were amber, like Philip's. Her nose was beaklike and her mouth was thin. Clawlike hands clutched at the arms of her chair, and her hunched body reminded Madeline of a bird of prey.

As Madeline and Philip entered the room Matterson, Lady Weatherby's trusted companion, was reading to her from the newspaper. But at a sign from Lady Weatherby the newspaper was quickly laid aside.

Madeline felt a shiver of apprehension as the dowager turned beady eyes on her, but nevertheless she lifted her chin. She had fought many battles in her short life, and if this proved to be another one then so be it.

'So. Found a way round your father's will at last?' Lady Weatherby demanded, fixing Philip with her penetrating glance. 'Never one to be led by the nose, were you, boy?'

'I take too much after you,' Philip said drily.

Lady Weatherby gave a cackle of laughter. 'A hit, boy. A palpable hit! And so,' she went on, turning her shrewd glance on Madeline, 'this is your new bride?'

'Yes. This is Madeline,' said Philip.

'Come closer, girl,' said the dowager, beckoning with one bony finger.

Madeline took a step forward, and felt the

dowager's eyes on her, scrutinizing her. 'So. Married m'nevvy, have you girl?'

'Yes, my lady.'

'Pretty manners, anyway,' she said judiciously. 'Pretty face, too. You've done us proud, m'boy,' she said to Philip. 'A lovelier countess there's never been, not even your great-grandmother, and she was one of the great beauties of her day.' The dowager turned her attention back to Philip. 'Well, no use sitting here all afternoon, not when there's sunshine outside. Ring the bell, Matty. Tell Crookshank we'll take tea on the lawn.'

The old lady rose to her feet and Philip offered her his arm. Then, offering Madeline his other arm they went outside, settling themselves beneath a spreading chestnut tree that grew in the middle of the well-kept lawn.

So far, the meeting had gone smoothly, thought Madeline. But remembering Philip's caution, she kept her wits about her. Although Lady Weatherby was being charming there was a sharp intelligence behind her eyes, and it was impossible to know what she was thinking.

Matty soon followed the small group with a pile of cushions which she arranged on the chairs that had been set under the tree, and tea was brought out. A silver tray was set on a wooden table spread with a snowy cloth and the beverage was poured from a silver teapot, fresh and hot.

To begin with, the time passed pleasantly. Lady Weatherby set herself out to entertain, and once they had finished their tea she regaled them with tales of her youth. 'D'you know what this reminds me of, Matty? This marriage of Madeline and Philip's?' she said, with a sly glance at Philip. 'With all the rumpus it's created it reminds me of the time Lady Caroline Lennox ran away with Henry Fox. You remember it, don't you Matty, old girl? It was the talk of the town.'

'Don't I just!' exclaimed Matty, as she arranged Lady Weatherby's cushions. 'I was in the schoolroom at the time, but my nurses were full of it. How romantic it sounded! And how daring! Imagine, defying the Duke of Richmond!'

'Duke of Richmond to you and me, but just her father to Lady Caroline,' snorted Lady Weatherby. 'Girls never have minded their fathers, and never will, I'll be bound.'

Madeline was startled. She had led an isolated childhood, and she had not realized that other girls defied their fathers. She had never even thought of defying her own father, but then, he had been such a bully that it was not surprising. As she listened to Lady Weatherby's tales she realized she knew very little about normal life. Perhaps, over the next six months, she would have a chance to learn.

'Still, it all turned out well in the end,' said Matterson, drawing Madeline's thoughts back to the present. 'Mr Fox became Lord Holland and Lady Caroline became Lady Holland. And she was reconciled with her family in the end.'

'Should think so, too,' snorted Lady Weatherby. 'No good breaking up a family just because of an odd hiccup here and there. And marriages do cause hiccups, as I should know!'

'My aunt married a man ten years her junior and scandalized the neighbourhood,' Philip explained to Madeline. 'He was just out of Oxford, and Aunt Honoria was an old maid.' His eyes twinkled as he said it, and Madeline guessed he was teasing his aunt.

'Old maid!' snorted Lady Weatherby, delighted to be given a chance to contradict. 'I was in my prime! Old maid, indeed! I was younger than you are now. Besides, I didn't create half the scandal you've created. Set London by the ears, you have. The Earl of Pemberton running off and getting married without even giving notice in *The Times*.'

'It will be a seven day wonder,' said Philip. 'Especially now, when the Season is almost over. By the time the *ton* return to the capital after the summer it will be old news, and some other scandal will have taken its place.'

'You're a cool one, I'll say that for you, nevvy,' said Lady Weatherby with a shrug of her bony shoulders. 'But I dare say you're right.'

★ ★ ★

'Such a pity the earl's marriage is only temporary,' sighed Matty sentimentally the following morning as she helped her mistress to dress. 'If only he wasn't in love with Miss Bligh.' She picked up the silver-backed hairbrush that lay on the dressing-table and proceeded to brush Lady Weatherby's still-glorious auburn hair.

'In love with that cold fish?' snorted Lady Weatherby. 'Philip isn't in love with Letitia. He thinks she'll make him a suitable wife, that's all.' A thoughtful look came into her eye, as she recalled Philip's behaviour towards Madeline. She had caught an expression on Philip's face in an unguarded moment that had given her food for thought. 'I wonder . . . Tell me, Matty, is Lord Fitzgrey still in residence?'

Lord Fitzgrey was an eligible bachelor who owned one of the neighbouring estates.

'I believe so,' said Matty, perplexed.

'Good. Send him an invitation,' said Lady Weatherby thoughtfully. 'Ask him to dinner.'

Matty was astonished. 'I thought you couldn't abide Lord Fitzgrey.'

'And so I can't. He's a damned jacka-napes,' said Lady Weatherby, not mincing her words. 'But a handsome one. And he has a way with women.'

'Is that wise, then?' asked Matty with a worried frown. 'What if he makes love to Madeline?'

'He'd better,' said Lady Weatherby shrewdly. 'That's why I'm inviting him.'

'But won't Philip object?' asked Matty, forgetting to brush her mistress's hair in her confusion.

'A hundred strokes!' commanded Lady Weatherby, reminding Matty of what she was meant to be doing. 'Will he object?' she repeated, her eyes shrewd, as Matty plied the silver-backed hairbrush once again. 'I don't know. That's what I want to find out.'

'Lord Fitzgrey may not accept an invitation at such short notice,' warned Matty.

'Hah!' snorted Lady Weatherby. 'As soon as he knows Philip's new bride's here, he'll come all right.' She paused as Matty twisted her hair into a chignon. 'You'd better invite the Carsons as well,' she added.

This time, Matty did not express doubts

about their willingness to attend. Mr Carson and his sister were great admirers of the nobility. They spent their time travelling from one fashionable spot to another, ingratiating themselves with anyone who possessed a title, and a dinner invitation from Lady Weatherby, no matter how short the notice, would always receive a positive reply.

* * *

The Carsons were the first to arrive that evening. Mr Carson was a small, spare man, but his sister was a large woman in every way. She was at least eight inches taller than her brother, and as her girth almost equalled her height she was an imposing sight. Dressed in purple satin she entered the room like a tent billowing in the breeze, and made straight for Lady Weatherby.

'My dear Lady Weatherby,' she said, making Lady Weatherby an extravagant curtsy, from which she had great difficulty rising again. She at last succeeded, however, and once firmly balanced again she said, 'What an honour it is to be invited to your table. Mr Carson and I are quite over-whelmed.'

Mr Carson professed himself similarly gratified by the invitation.

Lady Weatherby's eyes sparkled mischievously, but she welcomed the couple with otherwise perfect gravity.

'Good of you to come. Especially at such short notice,' Lady Weatherby said. 'May I present my nephew, the Earl of Pemberton?' she asked, introducing Philip.

'My Lord.' Miss Carson swept an even deeper curtsy. This time, however, she did not rise. Her smile became rigid, and it became apparent that her whalebone corsets had locked, freezing her into immobility.

Sensing her distress her brother sprang to her aid. A moment later, with his help, she rose like an inflating balloon and turned her attention to Madeline.

'And the Countess of Pemberton,' said Lady Weatherby, performing the introduction.

Miss Carson was about to sweep another extravagant curtsy when she thought better of it and contented herself with a modest bob. It was accompanied, however, by a most reverent bowing of the head.

Mr Carson then took Madeline's hand, bowing over it with equal reverence.

Madeline realized with relief that she had nothing to fear from the Carsons. She had been dreading the evening, in case a slip on her part gave away the nature of her marriage to Philip, but the Carsons were so over-whelmed by her rank that she was sure any small slips she might make would pass unnoticed.

The door opened again and the butler announced Lord Fitzgrey.

Madeline saw Philip cast a curious glance towards his aunt, but then she had to give her attention to the new guest.

Lord Fitzgrey could not have been more different from the Carsons. He was a handsome man of some twenty-seven or eight years old, dressed fashionably but unostenta-tiously in a blue tailcoat and a pair of knee-breeches. He wore many rings on his fingers, marking him out as a man of wealth and style. He greeted Lady Weatherby and Philip with easy affability, and then turned his full attention to Madeline.

And that was what he was giving her, Madeline realized. His full attention. He was treating her as though she was the only person in the room.

'I'm delighted to make your acquaintance, Countess,' he said, bowing over her hand. 'Pemberton,' he said, turning to Philip.

'Fitzgrey.' Philip returned his greeting. 'I didn't expect to see you here so late in the year. I thought you'd have gone down to Brighton as usual.'

There was an edge to his voice that Madeline did not understand.

'I will be going there shortly,' Lord Fitzgrey said. He turned back to Madeline. 'You have been to Brighton, of course, Countess?' he asked.

'No,' admitted Madeline.

'Then you must let me tell you all about it,' he said as dinner was announced.

'Fitzgrey, you'll take Madeline in.' said Lady Weatherby.

He turned appreciative eyes towards Madeline. 'I'd be delighted.'

Philip directed a sharp look in his direction, but then gave his arm to Miss Carson, whilst Mr Carson escorted Lady Weatherby, and the six of them moved through to the dining-room.

'Brighton is a wonderland,' said Lord Fitzgrey, as they settled themselves round the magnificent oak table. 'It has been a favourite haunt of the Regent's for many years.'

As he talked of the Regent's birthday celebrations, which were held there every August, the Regent's statue, which stood eighteen feet high, and the sea bathing, he appeared to be speaking to the entire table. But after the first few sentences of every new topic his eyes went exclusively to Madeline and stayed there. He helped her to wine, he handed her dishes and listened to her responses to his questions as though she was the only person in the room.

None of which escaped Philip's notice.

But why should Lord Fitzgrey not pay marked attention to Madeline? he asked himself as the meal continued. She was a new bride, and as such was the legitimate centre of attention.

But even so, having to sit there and make polite conversation with the Carsons whilst Fitzgrey monopolized Madeline made him seethe inside.

' . . . don't you think, my lord?'

Miss Carson's question brought his thoughts back to the conversation and he realized that he had heard barely a word of what she had been saying.

With difficulty he dragged his eyes away from Madeline and Fitzgrey and replied to Miss Carson.

'Quite,' he said; having no idea what she was talking about, no more intelligent reply was possible.

'And do you know,' went on Miss Carson, oblivious of the fact that he had not been listening to her transparent boasting, 'the Duchess was good enough to say that she thought my poor little emeralds were even prettier than hers?'

'How kind,' murmured Philip, his eyes drifting once again to Madeline and Fitzgrey.

'Yes, was it not?' she asked, delighted. 'Oh, look,' she exclaimed, as a confection of pastry and cream was brought in and set in the centre of the table. 'So elegant! So stylish! Why, it reminds me of the pastry tower we had at Lord Somerby's — you remember, Hector?' She turned to her brother appealingly.

'Indeed. Lord Somerby has an excellent chef,' he said. Then, realizing that praise for Lord Somerby's chef might not be welcome at Lady Weatherby's table, he turned to that lady and said, 'But not, dear Lady Weatherby, as good as your own.'

★   ★   ★

'It's such a shame the earl did not object to Lord Fitzgrey paying such marked attention to Madeline during dinner,' sighed Matty as she helped Lady Weatherby into bed later that night.

'He didn't object,' said Lady Weatherby shrewdly. 'But he didn't like it.' She gave a bark of laughter. 'He looked as though he was chewing nails!'

'And after all the effort Pierre had put into preparing the most delicious meal!' remarked

129

Matty. 'Lord Fitzgrey seemed very smitten,' she went on, as she tucked the covers round her mistress. 'What a shame he doesn't live in Yorkshire. Just think, if he did, then he could marry Madeline when her marriage to the earl is annulled.'

'Fool,' snorted Lady Weatherby, without, however, explaining exactly what she meant. 'Still, Fitzgrey's served his purpose,' continued Lady Weatherby thoughtfully. 'And this evening's given me an idea. Pass me my writing-case, Matty. I've a letter to send.'

6

There was a flurry of activity the following morning as the coach prepared to set out on the next stage of its journey. Lady Weatherby and Matterson stood at the top of the imposing flight of steps whilst a bevy of servants loaded the luggage, saw to the horses and filled the coach with small touches to make the journey pleasanter: a hamper of home-cooked food, a light travelling rug, and sweet-smelling sachets of herbs to freshen the air.

And then they were off.

'You seemed very taken with Fitzgrey,' said Philip, as he and Madeline travelled north.

'He was an agreeable gentleman,' said Madeline non-committally.

In fact she had not taken to him, but it would have been the height of bad manners to say so.

Hearing her answer, she saw a frown cross Philip's face but after apparently wrestling with himself for a moment he said no more.

Their journey continued as before. Days passed. As they went further north the landscape changed, becoming wilder and more open. Towns and villages were further apart, and in between there were expanses of wild moorland instead of cultivated fields. There was a harshness about the moors that Madeline had not come across before, the grass that covered them being tougher than the lush grass that grew in the low-lying fields, but despite its harshness she found it attractive. Here and there outcrops of rock thrust their way out of the landscape and twisted oak trees drew the eye. Lower down, away from the most exposed heights, sheep grazed.

And then at last they arrived in Yorkshire.

Since the masked men had held them up on the first stage of their journey they had not experienced any more unsettling incidents, and once in Yorkshire Philip allowed their pace to slow. With the gentler pace, Madeline spent more of her time in the saddle. She wanted to see her new home from horseback, the better to get to know it.

Philip often rode beside her, telling her about the various landmarks they passed, as well as the names of various towns and villages until at last he reined in his horse. Relations between them had been more cordial since their visit to Lady Weatherby, and their rapport had gradually returned; a rapport which would make it easier for them to convince Philip's friends and neighbours in Yorkshire that they were truly man and wife, Madeline told herself.

'This is the edge of the estate,' said Philip, turning towards her one morning as they reached the top of a steep incline and looked out across the open landscape. 'From here on, it is all Rochdale land.'

Madeline took in the vast panorama that lay ahead of them. All this belonged to Philip, she realized. And, for a short while, it belonged to her as well.

Philip turned to the coachman. 'Go on. The countess and I will ride across the moors for the rest of the way.'

'Yes, my lord.'

The man whipped up thc horses and the coach rolled forward.

'There is something I want to show you,' Philip said. 'We will reach it by way of this track.'

Madeline looked in the direction of his gaze and saw a small track leading across the moor, cutting through the swaths of purple heather that waved in the breeze.

Philip turned his horse's head and set out at a slow pace, guiding his own animal across the scrub and heather and leaving the track to Madeline's mare.

'Well, Madeline?' he asked as they picked

their way across the moors. 'What do you think of your new home?'

'I think it's beautiful,' she said, taking in the wild grandeur of the moors. 'It's so open I can see for miles.' As she said it she remembered how she had been hemmed in and trapped in London, and how it had oppressed her spirits. But here there was space in every direction.

'That's where we're heading,' he said, pointing ahead. 'That outcrop of rock on the horizon. It gives Stonecrop Manor its name. From there you can see the whole estate.'

The horses continued to pick their way across the fragrant moor until they reached the large outbreak of rock. It was set high up, and Madeline drank in the view.

'I can see why you love it,' she said.

Philip threw one leg over the back of his horse and dismounted, tying the reins to one of the rocks on the craggy outcrop.

'We'll stop here for a while. We still have a long way to go and you will need to rest.'

Madeline, tired from the day's exercise, readily agreed.

She reined in her horse.

Philip dismounted beside her and held out his arms to help her dismount.

Madeline hesitated. To be in his arms again — who knew what feelings it would produce?

But it had to be done. She certainly could not dismount without his help. Summoning her courage she sprang lightly from her mare's back and into his waiting arms, feeling his strong hands close round her waist. There was a momentary tingling sensation, and then to her relief he began to loose his grip. But as he did so a bird flew out of the heather and her mare took fright, pitching her forcefully forwards. Philip's arms tightened instinctively round her and she felt her body being crushed against his. She was suddenly so close to him that she could see every detail of his face: every line, every curve, every bristle that covered his chin. He was, with his scar, like a force of nature, rugged, indomitable, and powerful, his masculine scent harsh and exciting, at one with the unyielding landscape of rock and stone. If he kissed her now . . . her knees sagged with the thought and he caught her held her up, and then his lips closed over her own.

It was intoxicating. And when his tongue traced the line of her lips she was consumed by a rush of tingles that spread to the most intimate parts of her, arousing intense sensations the like of which she had never known. She should pull away, but she was too weak and too overcome by the feeling that she never wanted the kiss to end. Once it ended she would have to think; would have to wonder why it was she could bear him to touch her, let alone want him to caress her. She had never wanted any man near her before. Men disgusted her and made her afraid. But Philip . . . Her thoughts dissolved under the onslaught of the heady sensations that were coursing through her and she gave herself up to his kiss.

Finally he let her go. His eyes were filled with a gleam she had never seen before and it was matched by an answering fire in her own; but her mind was back in control now.

And so was his.

'You have my apologies, Madeline,' he said stiffly. 'That was unforgivable.'

It wasn't, she wanted to say, as she tried to swallow down the emotions that were still lighting her blood.

'You may rest assured it will never happen again,' he said.

Of course not, she thought as he walked away from her. He is not in love with me; he is in love with Letitia.

The thought gave her pain. She was under no illusions about the nature of her marriage to Philip. In fact, she would not have agreed to it had things been otherwise. It was only because it was a temporary marriage that she had felt able to be a party to it, because in that way she could be certain that her mother's unhappy fate would not become her own. Even so, she could not deny the feelings that he roused in her, feelings that were as wild and untamed as the moors themselves, feelings that had been created by the same ungovernable force: Nature.

And yet it was not just Nature.

At least not for her.

It was definitely something more.

That thought was too unsettling to pursue, so she walked in the opposite direction and sat down on an outcrop of rock. Her breathing began to return to normal, and as she grew calmer she was able to turn her thoughts away from Philip and take an interest in the landscape instead.

Below her the estate was spread out like a living map. In the distance, so far away and so far below her that it looked like a toy, was the manor. Around it was an expanse of green; and far off, flashing as it caught the sunlight, was a river, snaking its way through the fields.

'We should be on our way,' she called at last.

Philip, who had climbed the rocks that gave the estate its name, cast his hawklike gaze over his domain one more time, and then he gave up his place on the rocks and joined her.

Unwilling to let him touch her again, afraid

of her response, Madeline had already mounted. It had not been easy, but she had managed to use one of the rocks as a mounting block.

Together they set off towards the manor.

The landscape became gentler as they followed a path leading downwards, away from the exposed heights of the moors. The number of grazing sheep increased, and the sight of them cropping the grass created an atmosphere of pastoral tranquillity.

It was strange to think that somewhere Philip's friend was in danger, perhaps being pursued even now by the men who had held up the coach.

At last Madeline and Philip came to the manor. It was a splendid sight. Built entirely of pale golden stone, it was large and imposing. Windows were set at regular intervals along the walls, going down almost to the ground. They would give beautiful views over the gardens and fields beyond.

They rode up to the front door. Crump, in his element, was on hand to greet them.

As Madeline passed in through the high door she was surprised and somewhat alarmed to see that he had assembled all the servants to greet their master and their new mistress. For the first time, Madeline began to fully realize what being Philip's countess

— even his temporary countess — would mean. She lifted her chin. Although deception did not come naturally to her, circumstances had forced her to take on the role of Philip's wife and she meant to play her part.

'This is well thought of, Crump,' said Philip.

'It is only proper, my lord. The staff wished to pay their respects to Lady Pemberton.'

Philip nodded his approval. 'Well done.'

After a short speech of welcome, delivered by Crump in his most respectful manner, Philip said a brief word to each member of staff, before leading Madeline into the drawing-room.

'I don't think I've ever seen so many servants,' she remarked.

'It takes a lot of people to run a house of this size. But you need not worry about it. The servants will see to everything. You need do nothing more than amuse yourself.'

His manner was polite, but at the same time distant. The closeness of the previous weeks had vanished. It was as though, having realized he had overstepped the boundaries of their agreement by kissing her, he meant to make sure that nothing like that could ever happen again. And for that Madeline was grateful — or so she told herself. It had begun to mean too much to her, her rapport with Philip, and she must learn to let it go.

She looked round the room, glad of the excuse it gave her not to speak. She took in the elegant proportions and the tasteful furnishings. Venetian gilded mirrors hung on the walls and gilded chairs were scattered around the room. An elegant sofa upholstered in sage-green damask complemented the pale-green walls, and the white Adam fireplace gave the room a light and airy feel.

'And now I must leave you,' Philip said. 'I have been away from the estate too long as it is. If you need anything, Mrs Potts will be happy to help.'

'Mrs Potts?'

'The housekeeper.'

'But I thought Mrs Green . . . '

'Mrs Green is responsible for the London house. It is Mrs Potts who looks after the manor.'

'Of course.' Madeline realized once again how different the lifestyle of an earl must be from anything she had experienced. But she must learn, and learn quickly. Because now they had arrived in Yorkshire she would come under scrutiny from Philip's friends and neighbours, and she must be able to play her part convincingly.

If she did not, the true nature of her marriage to Philip would surely be discovered, and their six-month marriage would be over almost before it had begun.

7

'Well, my lady, things are looking up and no mistake,' said Jenny as she dressed Madeline's hair a few days later.

Madeline's bedroom was at the front of the house, overlooking the formal gardens, which Philip's father had designed himself.

'Perhaps,' said Madeline. Although the first few weeks of the marriage had passed well enough there were many months to go, and Madeline had not relaxed, as Jenny had. There had been the strange business of the break-in at the earl's London home, and then the incident with the masked men on the road, to say nothing of the confusing feelings Madeline had for Philip.

'The servants are a friendly lot. I thought they might be stuck up at first, but they've made me welcome,' said Jenny cheerfully. But then she gave a slight frown.

'What is it?' Madeline asked, happy to be drawn out of her own thoughts.

'Oh, nothing,' said Jenny with a shrug. 'It's just that one of the footmen, Danson, seems a bit . . . over friendly.'

'If you are having any trouble with him . . . '

'Oh, no, my lady, it's nothing like that,' said Jenny as she laced Madeline's corsets. 'He isn't too familiar, if that's what you're thinking. It's more that he's too interested, if you know what I mean. He asks too many questions. Where I'm from, how long I've been with you . . . ' And how you're getting along with the earl, Jenny thought, but did not say it. 'It's just a servant's nosiness, I dare say,' she continued. 'It's a bit out of the way here, my lady, not like London, where there's always plenty going on. He's just bored, most probably, and needs something to gossip about.'

'As long as you're sure he isn't bothering you,' said Madeline, looking at Jenny searchingly; for whilst Jenny was very protective of her mistress, Madeline was also protective of Jenny.

'Don't you worry your head about it,' said Jenny.

Madeline was satisfied, and turned her attention back to the gown that was laid out on her bed.

'Here, my lady, let me help you on with that,' said Jenny.

The gown was one of the first of Madeline's new dresses. It had been waiting for her on her arrival at the manor. It had been brought over by Miss Silverstone,

143

Madame Rouen's cousin, as soon as it was ready, and the other outfits were to follow when they were finished.

The dress was extremely beautiful. Madeline had resisted the idea of always dressing in silks and satins, as she had a feeling Madame Rouen would have liked her to have done, and had opted for a number of simple yet elegant day dresses, reserving the more luxurious fabrics for the outfits she would wear when she was out and about. The dress she now wore was of white muslin with a small jonquil spot. It was edged at the hem with a double-plaited ribbon in a matching shade, and a single-plaited ribbon marked out the high waist line and trimmed the puffed sleeves.

She looked in the cheval-glass to check that she was tidy before she went downstairs. She pushed one stray ringlet back from her face and smoothed her hand over the crown of her head, where her flaxen hair had been pulled back into a glossy chignon. She adjusted the handkerchief set into the scoop neckline of her gown and fastened a single strand of pearls round her neck. Then, after giving Jenny a few directions, she went downstairs.

On arriving at the manor she had at first felt overawed by the way Mrs Potts had looked to her for decisions about the running of the household, but to her relief she had found a collection of old household diaries in the pretty study that had been used by Philip's mother and had quickly realized they contained all the information she needed. Having read them through, she knew what had to be done in each week, and sometimes on each day, of the year, and could instruct Mrs Potts accordingly.

Once downstairs she went into the countess's study, a small and lovely room which overlooked the east side of the house. It was from here that Philip's mother had run the manor when she had been alive, and as all the servants were used to the arrangement Madeline had decided to continue with it, particularly as all the household diaries, account books and other necessary tomes were kept there.

She was just looking over the proposed menus for the week when Philip walked into the room.

'Mrs Potts told me I would find you here,' he said.

She waited for him to continue.

'The room is to your liking?' he asked. 'You have everything you need?'

He was being formally polite, as though there had never been anything but the cold arrangement of a six-month marriage between them. All the familiarity of their journey had vanished.

Try as she might to tell herself that she was grateful for it, Madeline knew that in reality she missed their former ease and companionability.

'Yes, thank you,' she said, answering him in similar vein.

'Good. Madeline,' he said. He stopped and then went on. 'After all that has happened over the past few weeks I have decided to provide you with a bodyguard.'

'A bodyguard?' she asked, surprised.

'Yes. There have been a number of unsettling incidents of late and I want to make sure you are safe when you go out riding on the estate.' He walked over to her and rested his hands protectively on her shoulders.

'Thank you, but that won't be necessary.' She had no desire for a bodyguard — her freedom had been too hard won — and she shrugged him off.

'It was not a request,' he said with a frown.

'Then what?' she asked. She spoke calmly, but her pulse was beginning to beat more quickly. She had been watched and hemmed in by her uncle in London, and she did not mean to let Philip, or anyone else, treat her in the same way. 'An order, perhaps?' She said it

146

lightly, but there was an underlying edge to her voice.

'Of course not,' he remarked.

'Then if it is not an order, I will decline.' She spoke calmly but with resolution.

'You need someone with you when you go out,' said Philip, his voice becoming as resolute as her own.

'I need no such thing.' She could feel her fear rising but she fought it down.

'Then perhaps it will be as well if you remained indoors,' he remarked.

'I will not be made a prisoner,' said Madeline, standing up and facing him. 'I will go where I want, when I want, and neither you nor anyone else will tell me otherwise.'

'And if you are attacked?' he demanded, his eyes boring into her own. 'What then?'

'I would rather face that possibility than have a bodyguard dogging my footsteps everywhere I go.'

'But I would not,' he returned.

He took her by the elbows, but again she shrugged him off.

'Then you must accustom yourself to it, because I will not be followed under any circumstances. And now, if you will excuse me, I have work to do.'

'Work?' he flared. 'I didn't bring you to Yorkshire to work.'

'Nevertheless, it is what I intend to do. There is a ball to be arranged — '

'Mrs Potts can do that,' he returned angrily.

'Mrs Potts needs a mistress to guide her.'

She glared at him. For a moment she thought he would continue to press her, but his anger fled as quickly as it had flared.

'I see you are determined,' he said icily.

'I am.' She lifted her chin defiantly.

'Then I will leave you to your own devices,' he said, tight-lipped.

He strode over to the door.

'Philip.'

He turned.

'Try and understand. I was hemmed in constantly by my uncle. I cannot be put under guard again.'

'You have made your position perfectly clear,' he said, before walking out of the door.

Leaving Madeline to wonder whether she had been a fool.

There *had* been dangers in London and on the journey north, she could not deny it. But surely those dangers had not followed them here?

She found herself glancing apprehensively out of the window, as though she expected to see a group of masked men burst out of the avenue of trees.

But nothing happened.

Of course not. The idea was ridiculous.

And telling herself to stop being fanciful, Madeline turned her thoughts back to the many things that needed her attention. There was the ball to be organized, and the preparations to be made for Emma's visit: Philip's sister was due to visit the manor for the summer holidays. And then there were a hundred and one other everyday affairs to be seen to.

Quite enough to do, without imagining further threats from masked men and mysterious break-ins, Madeline told herself. And without wondering why being on such bad terms with Philip had brought her close to tears. Sitting down once more at her desk she began to make a list of things she needed to do.

★   ★   ★

And why did I handle that so badly? Philip asked himself as he strode out to the stables and saddled his horse.

But he knew why. It was because Madeline was becoming increasingly important to him, and he couldn't bear to think of her being in danger. He had tried to fight it, the knowledge that, far from being an encumbrance who bored him with her idle chatter, as he had supposed she would be, Madeline was an intriguing and desirable young woman who set his blood on fire. But it was no use.

What then? Did he mean to overset all his plans?

Of course not. The notion was ridiculous.

It was not as though he was in love with her.

If he had been, there might have been a reason to question his choices. But as it was . . .

He rode out of the stable yard, and as he made for the open moorland he determinedly put all thoughts of Madeline out of his mind.

* * *

The following week passed quickly for Madeline. Together with Mrs Potts, she put preparations in hand for the ball. Although it was still some way off there was much to be organized, and the invitations had to be written and sent out in good time. In addition, she saw that Emma's room was cleaned and made ready for the young girl's visit.

At the end of the week, Philip said to her at dinner, 'I have to go in to York tomorrow. I have instructed Mr Greer to ready a number of houses for you so that you can choose the one you would like as your future home.'

Madeline had almost forgotten about the house in York. It had been part of her agreement with Philip that he would provide her with a house once their marriage had run its course, and it seemed he meant to keep to his promise.

She listened with interest as Philip outlined the houses he had chosen for her to see but instead of looking forward to seeing them she found that, for some reason, she was dreading it. She did not know why that should be. To have a house of her own, and an income to support herself, so that she need never be in anyone else's power again, had for a long time been her greatest desire. But for some reason it seemed to have lost its allure.

★ ★ ★

'There are a number of houses for you to visit this morning,' said Philip on the following day as they set out for York. 'The first house I want you to see is in St Leonard's Place. I think you'll like it. It has all the modern conveniences.'

As he spoke, the carriage turned a corner and rolled to a halt. Waiting for them on the

151

pavement was a round little man with an ingratiating smile.

'My lord, my lady,' he said, making a low bow as they stepped out of the carriage.

'This is Mr Greer,' said Philip, introducing Madeline to the manager of his York properties.

Mr Greer bowed lower still.

'Is everything ready?' Philip asked the little man as they went inside.

'Yes, my lord. The house has been opened up and aired, as you instructed, and the other houses are waiting for your inspection whenever you wish to see them.' He turned to Madeline 'This way, my lady.'

Together they looked over the house in St Leonard's Place. It was newly built and, as Philip had said, it had all the most modern conveniences. But for some reason Madeline did not take to it.

'What do you think of it?' asked Philip, as Madeline completed her inspection of the house.

'It's very nice,' she said.

Catching her tone of voice he said, 'But not the house for you. Never mind. It's only the first one on the list.'

They spent the morning looking at a number of other houses dotted around the city, until at last they came to the final one.

'This is a delightful house for you, if I may say so, my lady, when you want to spend a few days in York without the bother of going back to the manor every day,' gushed Mr Greer.

That was the reason that had been given to the manager for showing Madeline round a selection of houses: that the earl and his wife wanted a base in York, so that they could attend concerts or balls without having to face a long drive back to the manor afterwards.

The house was indeed delightful. It was rather small, but full of character. Large windows flooded the rooms with light, and there was even a distant view of the Minster. But although it was delightful, Madeline had no desire to live there.

'You don't look very happy,' said Philip as they completed their inspection of the house and went out to view the colourful garden. 'Do you not like it?'

'It's charming,' said Madeline, feeling that she was being ungrateful and trying to sound delighted.

'But?' asked Philip.

'But . . . do I have to decide today?' she asked suddenly.

Philip looked at her searchingly and then, as if reading at least a part of her feelings, said, 'No, of course not.' He turned to the manager. 'Thank you, Greer. We will let you know when we have made up our minds.'

'Very good, my lord.' The little man bowed them outside.

'Madeline . . . .'

Philip lifted his hand as though he were about to stroke her face.

She caught her breath.

But then his hand dropped to his side. 'Come. It's time for lunch.'

Lunch was taken in a private parlour at the Black Swan Inn. The inn, with its half-timbering, was an interesting one and the food was excellent. Madeline and Philip chose plain yet well-cooked fare: a dish of soup, a rib of beef, and a light syllabub for dessert. Then, much refreshed, they decided to take a walk down to the river.

Hardly had they reached it, however, when Madeline heard a cry of 'Philip!' and turning round she saw a young man hurrying towards them.

The young man had soft dark curls and magnificent clothes. He was dressed in the height of fashion, although to Madeline his dandified clothes looked slightly ridiculous. His shirt points were so high they must have made turning his head difficult, and his yellow pantaloons were garish, whilst his colourful waistcoat seemed to contain every colour of the rainbow. Still, he looked to be good-humoured, and Philip seemed pleased, rather than otherwise, to see him.

'Stuart!' he said.

'What a stroke of luck, bumping into you like this!' said the young man.

'Madeline, may I introduce my cousin, Stuart.'

'So this is the lovely Madeline,' said Stuart, bowing over her hand.

'What brings you to York?' asked Philip, as Stuart seemed disinclined to let go of Madeline's hand.

'Oh, this and that. Business, you know,' said Stuart cheerfully, as he pulled his eyes away from Madeline.

'Business?' Philip raised one eyebrow. 'What kind of business?'

'Oh, one thing and another,' said Stuart vaguely. 'But I see you're all set for a walk by the river. Splendid! I was just going to take a stroll myself.'

'How long are you staying in York?' asked Philip as the three of them walked on together.

'Oh, a while, I dare say,' said Stuart breezily. 'Nothing to get back to town for, you know. It's so much pleasanter up here in Yorkshire in the summer. By the way,' he said casually, 'Aunt Honoria asked me to send you her love.'

'You've seen Aunt Honoria?' asked Philip in surprise.

Madeline had the feeling that it was unusual for the young man to visit his aunt.

'Why not? I get out there now and again, you know,' said Stuart, though he seemed a trifle uncomfortable as he said it.

'And how did you find her?'

'Oh, as well as ever. I must say, she does ever so well. Never seems to get any older. Bright as a button.' He gave a strangely self-satisfied smile. 'She tells me you're holding a ball,' he added conversationally. 'I must say I think it's a good idea. That way everyone can meet Madeline and welcome her to the manor,' he said with a bow in Madeline's direction.

'That's right.' Philip's voice did not sound encouraging.

'When is it?' asked Stuart casually.

'Oh, not for some time. These things take a while to arrange.'

'I dare say I'll still be around,' said Stuart carelessly.

There was a pause. But before it could become uncomfortable Philip said, 'You'll be welcome, of course.'

'Good,' said Stuart heartily. 'I'll look forward to it.'

Stuart entertained them with stories of the Regent's latest extravagances, until at last Philip said, 'Time for us to be getting back.'

'And I must be going, too,' said Stuart. 'I've got an appointment with my tailor. It was good to meet you, Madeline,' he said, taking her hand again as he made his farewells. Once again she was conscious of a certain inexplicable tension in Philip as Stuart held on to her hand for a moment longer than necessary. And then they parted.

'He seems like a pleasant young man,' said Madeline cautiously as she and Philip made their way back into town.

'Does he indeed,' said Philip darkly. Then, seeming to remember himself, he said, 'But now, you will be wanting to collect your riding-habit. I will take you to Miss Silverstone's and then I must attend to my own business affairs before we return to the manor.'

Once arrived at the modiste's, Madeline was pleased to discover that her clothes were progressing well. Her ball-gown would need only one more fitting and her riding-habit was all but finished. It only needed the last of the trimmings sewing on and then it would be delivered the following day.

Philip soon rejoined her and then, their errands done, they set out for home.

The distance between York and Stonecrop was a comfortable one. They had a pleasant drive through the Yorkshire countryside before turning in between the imposing gates that marked the entrance to the manor. Madeline was just thinking with satisfaction of her new riding-habit when the peace of the afternoon was shattered as a loud shot rent the air.

'What the . . . ?' exclaimed Philip.

Madeline looked at him in alarm. But there was no time to worry about the shot, because they had a much more immediate problem. The horses had taken fright at the sudden noise and the coach began to sway as the animals bolted. Madeline clasped the leather strap that hung from the carriage roof and clung on as they went faster and faster, with the coach lurching from side to side. She heard the cries of the coachman as he called out to the horses in an attempt to steady them and then Philip, bracing himself against the side of the carriage, pulled her roughly towards him, enfolding her in his arms, as he said through clenched teeth, 'We're going over.'

Madeline felt the carriage turning on to its side, and felt Philip's arms closing more

158

tightly about her as he shielded her with his body. There was an almighty bump and she felt herself thrown as the carriage rolled over. The world seemed to turn upside down; and then . . . calm.

'Are you all right?' Philip, thrown on top of her by the accident, raised himself on his elbows and looked down at her in concern. 'Madeline?'

'Y . . . yes.' She recovered her wits, which had been badly shaken, and said more definitely, 'Yes.'

'We need to get out of the carriage. It could roll over again.' He looked up at the carriage door, which was now on the roof, as he spoke, and reaching out one hand he hauled himself up until he could open it. Then, pulling himself out, he braced himself against the side of the carriage and lifted Madeline out after him.

'The coachmen . . . ' she said.

Philip glanced briefly at the men, who had been thrown clear, and who were even now catching and calming the terrified horses. 'They're all right,' he said. He called one of them over to him. 'See the countess safely back to the manor, Bates,' he instructed the man. Then, turning to Madeline, he went on, 'I'll join you shortly.'

Without waiting for her to reply he caught

one of the carriage horses. Removing enough of its harness and trappings to make it fit to ride he threw his leg over its back and galloped off in the direction of the shot.

Madeline felt a touch of fear as she watched him go. She did not know exactly what had just happened but she suspected it had something to do with Philip's friend: the spy.

'Don't worry, my lady,' said the elderly coachman. 'The earl knows what he's doing. It'll take some time to right the carriage,' he went on, shaking his head as he looked at the overturned vehicle. 'Will you wait here until we've managed it, or shall I send to the manor for your mare, my lady?'

'No.' Madeline shook her head. 'It isn't far.' She glanced at the manor, which was no more than half a mile away. 'I'll walk.'

'Very good, my lady,' he said, preparing to walk with her.

'I'll be perfectly all right by myself,' she said. If a gunman was really on the loose then an unarmed escort would not be of any help against him, and the coachman was needed to help catch the remaining horses and right the carriage.

'The earl said — '

'The shot was fired well away from the house,' Madeline said, looking behind her to the open moorland from where the sound had come. 'I will not be in any danger. You are needed here.'

The coachman looked dubious.

'You have your instructions,' said Madeline, injecting a note of authority into her voice. 'See to the carriage and the horses.'

The man hesitated for the merest instant before touching his hat and saying, 'Yes, my lady.'

Madeline had not known whether he would obey her new instructions but evidently her logic, together with her tone of authority, had persuaded him.

She set off along the drive. It was pleasantly cool now that the sun had almost gone down, and she found herself enjoying the walk. The exercise was beneficial and soon began to calm her overwrought nerves. But as her body grew calmer, her mind grew more active. What had been the meaning of the shot? Who had fired it? Why had they done so? Had they been shooting at someone in particular? And if so, who?

Was Philip in any danger? Though she was worried about him, she had to admit to herself that it did not seem likely. The shot had not been fired at him, but had instead been fired some distance away from him.

What then? Had the shot really some

connection to the man who had saved Philip's life? She had thought so at first. But perhaps she was mistaken. Perhaps it had had a more mundane cause. It might simply have been fired by a poacher trying to bag a bird.

She shook her head. She had no way of knowing what had really happened, and it was useless to think about it.

She was endeavouring to put it out of her mind when she heard the sound of hoofbeats galloping towards her. She turned round, expecting to see that Philip had returned, but instead she saw a total stranger riding towards her on a foaming black mount. His hair was long and his clothes were badly stained. There was a look of wildness about him as he hurtled towards her. His eyes were fixed and his hair was flying behind him in the breeze.

For a moment Madeline froze. And then she began to run. Before realizing that running in front of a horseman who was almost upon her would be useless, as she would never be able to outrace a horse. She stopped and looked around for cover. But too late! The horseman reined in his horse in one assured movement and leapt to the ground in front of her. She stepped back . . . then stood stock still in amazement as, instead of attacking her, he swept off his hat and made her an extravagant bow.

'My apologies, Countess,' he said with a laugh, his teeth gleaming and his eyes dancing. 'I didn't meant to startle you. Jack Saunders at your service.' He straightened up and his eyes glanced merrily over her. 'You *are* the Countess of Pemberton?' he asked.

Madeline could do nothing but nod mutely, still too stunned to speak.

'Funny, I thought . . . ' he said, seeming to remember that Philip had talked of marrying Letitia Bligh. 'But no matter. I am delighted to meet you. I wanted to speak to Philip, but as I can't wait for him to get back and as I have no desire to follow him — he has ridden off in the direction of my pursuers and I've no intention of getting caught! — I will ask you to give him this.'

He drew a crumpled piece of paper out of his pocket and handed it to Madeline.

'Tell him, if he doesn't hear from me again by the end of the week, he's to get this to Callaghan with all speed.'

Madeline took the piece of paper. Despite his unkempt appearance there was something so appealingly roguish about the man who stood before her that she had no hesitation in promising to do as he asked.

'I'll give it to him as soon as I see him,' she said.

163

'Thank you.' He made her another extravagant bow and then, seizing her hand, he planted a kiss on it before springing back on to his horse and galloping away.

Madeline watched his retreating figure until it was no more than a speck in the distance. Unless she mistook the matter entirely, she had just met the man who had saved Philip's life.

Once he had disappeared from view she turned her attention to the crumpled piece of paper. What could be so important that a man would be willing to risk his life for it? she wondered.

But before she had time to smooth it out and look at it properly she heard another thudding of hoofs and realized Philip must have returned. She looked up . . . only to see a second stranger bearing down on her. Icy fingers clutched at her insides. Although this man was clean shaven and well dressed, there was something about him that made the hairs stand up on the back of her neck. This time, however, she had more of a head start. She hesitated for only a second and then she turned and ran. If she could just get near enough to the manor to he seen, then the servants would come to her aid. But the hoofs were getting louder. They were thrumming in her ears. She looked over her shoulder, and saw the man's arm outstretched to grasp her. Instinctively she ducked . . . and felt his arm snatch at the empty air over her head. She heaved a sigh of relief as he galloped past. But then, to her horror, she saw him wheel his mount and charge straight towards her again.

Her heart began to hammer in her chest. She must get away.

And then she heard a shout behind her and, looking round, saw Philip, his face grim, riding towards her hell for leather, his coat-tails streaming behind him in the wind.

Two horses, one in front, one behind, on a collision course, and she was in the middle. She must move, spring aside . . . Without conscious thought she threw herself out of the way of the two beasts, leaving them to pass within an inch of each other. As they did so Philip took one hand off the reins and in a single fluid movement struck his adversary a powerful blow across the chest. The stranger fell, a look of fury on his face, already beginning to roll as he hit the ground . . . but he struck a large stone with his head as he fell and he did not get up again.

Philip leapt from his horse and went over to his fallen adversary, making sure the man was truly unconscious, before rounding on Madeline.

'What the devil do you think you're doing,

walking back to the manor on your own?'

His voice was thunderous.

'Bates was needed to see to the carriage and catch the horses. I saw no need to take him with me.'

'I gave orders — '

'And I countermanded them.'

'You had no right . . . ' he began, seething.

'I am the Countess of Pemberton! I had every right,' flashed Madeline. 'Besides, what good could Bates have done against armed and mounted men?'

'This isn't a picnic,' he said, grasping her elbows, his eyes boring into her own. 'These men are killers. The next time I tell you to do something, you do it. Do you understand?'

'Are you attempting to give me orders?' she demanded, beginning to shake. Her father had given her mother orders. Her uncle had given her orders. She had thought Philip was different.

'Damn it, Madeline,' he said. 'There's a time when orders are necessary. You should know that, having seen what you've just seen.'

She was about to make a hot reply when there was a rumbling noise. Unseen and unheard by either of them, the coach had been righted and was pulling up alongside them.

Philip let go of Madeline's elbows and

turned to Bates. 'I thought I told you to escort the countess back to the manor,' he said to the coachman angrily as the man reined in the horses.

'It is not his fault,' Madeline returned. 'As I have already told you, I ordered him to see to the carriage.'

'Then now that it has been righted I suggest you avail yourself of it,' said Philip curtly. And bundling her inside he said sharply to the coachman, 'Take the countess back to the manor. And do not accept any countermanding of my orders ever again. Do you understand me?'

'Yes, my lord,' said Bates with a gulp. He whipped up the horses and the carriage pulled away.

And why did I overreact like that? thought Philip angrily to himself as the carriage rumbled off down the drive. From the moment I first set eyes on Madeline I have wanted to protect her, and yet I have just berated her in the most unforgivable way.

But he knew why he had done it. He had done it because the thought of Madeline being hurt had terrified him.

Because without Madeline he could not claim his fortune, he told himself. But he knew even as he thought it this was not the real reason he had been afraid.

He did not want to pursue that thought. Instead he sat watching the carriage as it rolled towards the manor. Then, drawing his thoughts with difficulty back to the present, he slung the unconscious body of his adversary over the man's horse, mounted his own animal and followed the carriage back to the manor.

★   ★   ★

'Will you be so good as to tell the earl I must speak to him urgently when he returns?' Madeline asked Crump as she swept into the hall. 'I will be in my room.'

'Yes, my lady,' said Crump.

Madeline went upstairs. To her annoyance, she found that she was shaking.

Why had Philip been so angry? Why had he given her orders? Why had he behaved like her father and her uncle, when she had thought he was different?

He is different, said a small voice inside her. He is not angry with you because he wants to hurt you. He is angry because he cares.

But that thought was too disturbing to contemplate, and she pushed it from her mind.

Once in her room she rang for Jenny. The

accident had left her dirty, and she wanted to clean and freshen herself before going downstairs to see Philip.

She removed her cape and bonnet, then noticed that her dress was torn. Really, it was not surprising. She had been thrown about so much in the carriage it was a wonder the damage was not worse.

Jenny soon arrived, gasping, 'Oh, my lady, what has happened?' as she entered the room.

'Nothing,' said Madeline reassuringly. 'A slight accident, that's all.'

'I'd best fetch hot water,' said Jenny, suiting her actions to her words.

She returned not long afterwards with a jug of hot water and poured it into the bowl, then set about helping Madeline to undress.

'Your arms!' exclaimed Jenny.

Madeline looked down. A number of bruises were beginning to show.

'I'd better have another gown with long sleeves,' said Madeline, relieved that the weather was cool so that she would be able to disguise the bruises. 'The spotted muslin, I think.'

'Very good, my lady.'

Jenny laid the spotted muslin on the bed. She helped Madeline to sponge herself down and then eased her into the pink-spotted gown.

'That's much better,' said Madeline with relief. No one would now guess she had been in an accident.

'I'll just see to your hair, my lady,' said Jenny. She unpinned Madeline's chignon, which was already falling down, and then said in concern, 'Your forehead, my lady.'

Madeline looked in the glass. There was a long cut on her forehead. It was not serious, but it needed to be bathed.

'How did it happen?' asked Jenny as she poured a basin of clean water and then sponged away the dried blood. 'I thought you went out in the carriage. Did it overturn?'

'Unfortunately, yes.' Madeline described how the horses had bolted; without, however, mentioning the shot as she saw no need to alarm Jenny.

Jenny had fortunately heard nothing about the accident in the servants' hall, as it had happened so recently, and so she did not ask any awkward questions. She simply busied herself with seeing to Madeline's cut, and then announced that she had done.

Madeline examined her forehead in the mirror and was relieved to see that it was no longer bleeding.

'If I tease out a few more ringlets,' said Jenny thoughtfully, 'they should cover the cut, my lady.' Deftly she rearranged the ringlets that framed Madeline's face, brushing them carefully until they hid the cut, then stood back.

'That's much better,' said Madeline, surveying the results. 'Thank you, Jenny.'

Dressed in her clean spotted muslin gown, and with her hair neatly rearranged, Madeline felt better able to face Philip; they had parted on bad terms, and something told her there would be more difficulties to come.

She straightened the neckline of her gown, picked up her fan and reticule, and went downstairs.

'The earl will be with you directly, my lady,' said Crump, meeting Madeline in the hall. 'He has caught a poacher, and is making arrangements for the man's detention.'

A poacher? thought Madeline in surprise, before realizing that Philip must have invented a story about a poacher to conceal the truth, as the truth might well alarm the neighbourhood.

Madeline went through in to the drawing-room, where a few minutes later Philip joined her.

She could see at once that his good humour had not been restored. However, she could not put it off any longer. She must hand over Jack's message without delay.

'I would like to speak to you, my lord,' she

171

said, as Philip did not say anything.

His manner was curt. 'So Crump said.'

'I would not trouble you if it was not important,' she said, angered by his attitude.

'Very well.' He sat down on the edge of a Hepplewhite chair. 'I'm listening.'

'I have something for you.'

His look seemed to imply that nothing she could give him would interest him.

She took the crumpled piece of paper out of her reticule and held it out to him. 'It is from Jack.'

At once he was alert. 'Jack?' He all but snatched the piece of paper from her, standing up as he did so. 'From Jack, you say?' he asked, as though he suspected he had not heard her aright.

'Yes. Jack Saunders.'

'But how . . . ?' he began.

'He rode up to me when I was walking back to the manor. He leapt off his horse and handed me the piece of paper. It was you he wanted to see, but you were too close to his pursuers and he did not want to risk getting caught, so he followed me instead. He gave me the piece of paper you are now holding. He said, if he hasn't contacted you by the end of the week, you're to give it to Callaghan. Does that make sense to you?'

Philip smoothed out the piece of paper and

172

studied it thoughtfully. 'It might do.' He looked at her. 'What makes you say the man you saw was Jack?'

'He introduced himself.'

'That means nothing,' said Philip with a frown. 'Anyone could claim to be Jack and you wouldn't know the difference. This may be false information. Tell me exactly what this 'Jack' did and said.'

'He leapt off his horse, swept off his hat, and made me a low bow,' said Madeline, remembering. Then he said, 'My apologies, Countess. I didn't mean to startle you. Jack Saunders at your service.' Then he gave me the piece of paper and asked me to give it to you.'

'Did he say anything else?'

Madeline shook her head. 'He did not have time. He simply kissed my hand and then sprang back on his horse.'

'It certainly sounds like Jack,' said Philip with an unwilling smile. 'Only Jack would take the time to kiss your hand if he was being pursued. And then?'

'And then he rode away. Just before the other man bore down on me.' She looked at Philip defiantly, half expecting him to rail at her again for having disobeyed him by walking back to the manor alone. But he did not do so.

Neither, however, did he offer her an apology for his earlier outburst.

Instead he seemed to have forgotten all about it. Engrossed in examining the crumpled piece of paper, he seemed to have forgotten about her, too.

Without looking at her or speaking to her again he turned on his heel and walked out of the room.

★ ★ ★

Not an hour later Philip was in his study, sitting at his desk. In front of him stood a capable-looking man in rough clothes, who looked halfway between a workman and a bruiser.

The last time he had offered Madeline a bodyguard she had refused one, recalled Philip. But the idea of her being hurt was too terrible to contemplate, and after this last dangerous episode he did not intend to give her a choice.

'Jenkins,' said Philip, 'I have a job for you. A delicate job.' He looked at the man appraisingly, then asked, 'You've heard what happened here this afternoon, I take it?'

'Yes, my lord.'

'Good. Then I don't need to brief you on the . . . disturbance, shall we say. There is a

174

possibility that something like it may happen again, and I want to make sure that whatever happens the countess is safe. I want you to watch over her. You are to follow her every time she leaves the manor, and you are never to let her out of your sight. Do you understand?'

'Yes, my lord.'

'That part of the job is easy enough. It is the next part that is difficult. The countess objects to being followed. Therefore you must make sure that she never catches sight of you. You must be her shadow, but an invisible one. Follow her, but discreetly.' He remembered her treatment at the hands of her uncle, but whilst he understood her objections to being followed, he was no longer prepared to risk her safety. 'I don't want her to feel watched or hemmed in,' he cautioned the man.

'I understand, my lord.'

'Good. If the countess is ever in any danger it is your job to make sure she returns to the manor safely. Nothing else matters. You are not to chase her pursuers, nor to leave her unguarded for any other reason. The countess's safety is your priority at all times.'

'Yes, my lord.'

'Very good. Oh, and one other thing, Jenkins,' he said, as the man was about to leave. 'Make sure you are armed.'

'Yes, my lord.' Jenkins bowed and withdrew.

Philip went over to a locked cupboard at the side of the room and took out a pair of pistols. He did not know exactly what was going on but he knew that Jack was intending to return to Stonecrop, if he could, within the week, and if Jack was intending to return then his pursuers might well return also and Philip meant to be prepared.

He loaded both pistols and put them back in the cupboard, then drew out again the piece of paper Jack had given to Madeline. It contained two names: Tythering and Peters.

The first name meant nothing to him. But the second . . . He thought of the man he had captured in the driveway, who was now under guard in one of the barns. Whilst the man had still been unconscious Philip had gone through his pockets and found a letter addressed to Crispin Peters. It had not been conclusive: the letter did not necessarily belong to the man himself. But when he had come round Philip had addressed him as Peters and he had responded.

Peters. Crispin Peters.

Philip glanced at the piece of paper once more.

Jack had asked him to get the names to Callaghan, if he did not make contact within the week. But Philip intended to go one better. He did not simply intend to take the names of the two men on Jack's list to Callaghan. He also intended to take one of the men.

8

It was with relief that Madeline saw a carriage draw up in front of the house on the following morning. The atmosphere had been tense since the incident on the previous day, and she hoped a visitor would help to restore more amicable relations between Philip and herself. If they were to live together for the next few months then a cordial atmosphere was necessary, particularly if they were to convince everyone that they were a happily married man and wife.

The visitor was Clarissa Rogers, the rector's daughter. Clarissa was a spinster of some five-and-thirty years of age, and she was both good natured and good humoured. She had made Madeline feel most welcome on her arrival in Yorkshire and had told her a lot about the neighbourhood — the sort of things that Philip was less interested in, or less informed about, such as which young lady was about to leave the schoolroom, or which matron was expecting a child — helping Madeline to feel at home. Clarissa had accompanied her father when he had called on Madeline on her first day at the manor, but this morning she had arrived without the rector, and instead had two strangers in tow.

'My dear Countess, I came as soon as I heard,' said Clarissa, going over to Madeline and taking her hands. 'A shocking business. These poachers. Firing shots and scaring horses and overturning carriages — monstrous!' She finally paused to draw breath.

Of course! thought Madeline. Clarissa had heard of the disturbance at the manor, and delighting in innocent gossip, had decided to pay a call. Luckily, Clarissa appeared to have accepted the story about a poacher, which Philip had put abroad.

'Good morning, Miss Rogers,' said Philip.

'Oh, yes, good morning, my lord! Goodness, where are my manners? I was so concerned for Madeline that I almost forgot to greet you. But yes, my lord, good morning indeed! And it is a good morning, if dear Madeline is all right.' She looked at Madeline anxiously. 'You are all right, are you not?'

'Never better,' said Madeline comfortingly.

'Oh! That is such a relief.' Clarissa untied the strings of her bonnet and then, catching sight of the couple who had followed her into the room, said, 'Goodness! I am forgetting everything this morning. Madeline — Countess — may I present to you my brother, Percival, and his wife, Amelia. They are

179

paying us a visit at the rectory.'

Madeline felt a slight frisson of fear as Clarissa introduced Percival and his wife. The only marriage she had seen, the only real marriage, had been the marriage of her parents, and she assumed that all marriages would be equally dreadful. As she took in Percival, a stout gentleman of some forty years of age, she felt sorry for Amelia, as she anticipated the belittling remarks Percival would address to his wife during the course of the visit. But to her surprise, Amelia did not seem to share her dread. Instead of looking pale and drawn, Amelia looked alert and happy instead.

Once divested of their outer clothes, Clarissa, Amelia and Percival took the seats offered to them and as Clarissa continued to condole with her on her accident, Madeline could not help her gaze wandering to Amelia and Percival again. She found their attitude to each other surprising. No matter how hard she looked for it, Madeline could detect no trace of fear in Amelia's voice when she spoke to Percival. Indeed, Amelia seemed to have no fear of her husband at all. And as the conversation went on, ranging over a wide variety of topics that were of local interest, Madeline had to admit there seemed no reason for Amelia to fear him. He was kind, gentle and polite. He didn't belittle Amelia. He seemed to genuinely welcome his wife's ideas, and he and Amelia often exchanged a kind but humorous look as Clarissa's garrulous tongue ran away with her. But why? Madeline could understand why Philip was on occasion kind to *her*, as she was helping him to claim his inheritance. But she couldn't understand why Percival would be kind to Amelia. Percival's marriage was real, and he therefore had no reason to treat Amelia well. He had already taken charge of her dowry, and had nothing more to gain. And it was when men had taken charge of their wives' dowries — when they had nothing more to gain — that their cruelty started, as her mother had tragically told her. But Percival's cruelty, it seemed, had not started. And if it had not started by now, surely it never would?

Could marriages actually be happy? wondered Madeline. She would not have believed it, but she had the evidence of it before her own eyes. She thought of her mother and father again, and for the first time she asked herself whether their marriage had been the exception rather than the rule.

' . . . do you not agree, Countess?' asked Clarissa.

'Wool-gathering?' asked Philip wryly, seeing

181

Madeline start as she gathered her wandering thoughts.

'I'm afraid so,' she admitted ruefully.

'It's not to be wondered at, after the shock you had yesterday,' said Clarissa consolingly.

The accident was much discussed, and afterwards the conversation turned to the war and other topics of the day. When at last there was a lull in the conversation Percival directed a meaningful look at his sister.

'Yes, of course,' said Clarissa. 'We have kept you far too long, Madeline, and we must leave you to rest, but I am so glad to have seen you. It is such a relief to know that you are all right.'

'Will you be staying in Yorkshire for long?' asked Philip, as Percival and Amelia stood up.

'A few weeks, I hope,' said Percival.

'Then you will join us at our ball?'

Amelia and Percival expressed themselves delighted to accept the invitation before taking their leave with Clarissa.

Madeline gave an inaudible sigh of relief. Their visit had done much to dispel the tension that had filled the manor since the previous evening, and she felt that she and Philip would now be able to talk to each other without open hostility. In fact, Philip seemed on the verge of speaking to her even now.

But instead he frowned as his eyes suddenly fixed themselves on her forehead. Despite the fact that Madeline had arranged her hair differently in order to cover the cut, he had noticed it. 'I didn't realize you had been injured yesterday,' he said.

'It's nothing,' said Madeline. 'When the carriage overturned I was slightly scratched, that's all.'

He lifted his hand and pushed aside her ringlets, as if to reassure himself that the cut was indeed slight. Then he ran his hand over the smooth crown of hair. She felt the pressure of his fingers and instinctively turned her head back and forth, the better to feel his touch. He lifted his other hand and unravelled her glossy chignon, running his fingers through her flaxen hair like a comb.

The feel of them against her scalp was soothing and stimulating both at once. She gloried in his touch, wondering how it could produce such tantalizing sensations, and wishing it could never end.

But then his fingers stilled. He took her chin between them and turned her face up to his, looking deeply into her eyes.

Her breath caught in her throat.

He held her so for a heart-stopping moment, but then, as if coming to his senses, he released her chin and took a step back. 'I have made a mess of your hair, I fear,' he said.

'Never mind.' She tried to appear calm, as though it was an everyday occurrence for him to loosen her hair and run his fingers through it, but even so her voice was breathless. 'Jenny will soon put it right.'

He looked as though he wanted to say something further. But then a formal mask came down over his face and he walked out of the room.

★　★　★

Madeline saw little of Philip over the following week. He had a lot of business to attend to on the estate, and then he had to make a trip to London to deliver Jack's message, as well as Peters, to Callaghan.

Jack himself had not been seen again.

Madeline, too, was very busy. First of all she decided on one of the York properties; though she did not relish the decision, she realized she could not put it off. Then she spent her time organizing flowers, food and musicians for the ball, frequently consulting the old countess's diaries so that she did not forget to make any of the arrangements necessary for such a grand occasion.

At last nearly everything was ready. It had

helped, of course, that Mrs Potts had already made a few preliminary preparations, and that the neighbourhood had been expecting the ball; if not for that fact everything would have taken far longer to arrange. But local tradesmen had been holding themselves ready, knowing what would be required of them, and the county gentry had kept their diaries clear.

The one disappointment was that Emma, Philip's sister, had a slight indisposition and was not well enough to travel. She had spent the early part of her holiday from the Bath seminary, where she was a pupil, with her aunt and uncle, who lived in Bath, but she had been meaning to travel to Yorkshire once Philip and Madeline had settled into the manor. But now she would not be able to join them for the time planned. She would, however, visit them as soon as she was well enough, and Madeline was pleased that her visit had been simply delayed instead of cancelled: she was looking forward to meeting the young girl.

On the day before the ball, preparations were so well in hand that Madeline took the opportunity for a ride. Her habit, a delightful outfit of dark blue decorated with gold frogging, was ready, and had been hanging in her wardrobe for some time. She had been wary of going out by herself after the incident with the horseman, and had even considered telling Philip that she had changed her mind about having a man with her to protect her, but as the days had passed her confidence had returned, and she now enjoyed riding on the estate without anyone in attendance; she had had so many people watching her when she had lived with her uncle, and all of them paid to act as her gaolers, that now she loved to be free. And besides, she wanted to see the cottages that Philip meant to replace.

Although he was kept busy, Philip liked to discuss his plans for the estate with Madeline, and in the evenings they spent many enjoyable hours talking over a variety of ideas. One of these ideas had been for the replacement of a group of cottages which were badly damp, and Madeline wanted to see the problem for herself.

She went down to the stables and before long she was on her way, riding on her white mare. It took her a little over half an hour to reach the cottages and once there she dismounted, tethering her mare to a stunted tree.

A little boy, drawn by the noise of the horse's hoofs, ran out of the middle cottage, and stood staring at her. It was not an insolent stare, more an interested one, and she guessed he did not see very many people, and certainly not many ladies. A man followed him and stood behind him, resting his arms over the boy's shoulders.

The man nodded, and said, 'Areet.'

This, Madeline had learned, was a greeting, meaning, she supposed, 'All right', which in turn seemed to be short for 'I hope you're all right'. Or, as she would have put it, 'I hope I find you well'. And so she had explained it to Jenny, who had gone into peals of laughter and had had to wipe the tears of laughter from her eyes with her apron.

'Good morning,' she said in reply.

She had found that the 'Yorkshire folk' did indeed speak a strange dialect, but she had also found that most of them could make themselves understood when they wanted to. The dialect, she suspected, was a useful way of keeping outsiders at bay.

The people themselves she had found to be friendly once their initial hostility had worn off. They had looked at her suspiciously to begin with, as though they had expected her to start telling them how to cook their dinners and how to dress their children. But once they had discovered she was interested instead of interfering they had become welcoming.

The man before her, however, was

unknown to her as she had not ridden out this way before. She knew from experience that it would take a while before he began to accept her.

'I wanted to see the cottages,' she explained. 'The earl has told you of his plans to rebuild them, I understand?'

The man nodded, being neither friendly nor unfriendly, as if he was summing her up.

'I was wondering whether I might have a look inside.'

The man was silent. Then he stood aside and let her go in.

'Shall you be pleased to see the cottages rebuilt?' she asked.

The man shrugged. 'I reckon they need summat doing.'

'Summat doing?' came a woman's voice, and a minute later a buxom, red-faced woman came down the stairs. 'I'll say they need summat doing. As damp as anything in the winter, they are, and the chimneys won't draw. The old earl would've done summat, but he lost heart after the old countess died.' She looked at Madeline as her husband had, as if summing her up, then nodded. 'I reckon you'll do.'

Many countesses would have been horri-fied at this last remark, but Madeline was impressed by the Yorkshire people's honesty.

They liked to speak their minds, and out here in the wilds of Yorkshire, away from the polish — and the insincerity — of London, it seemed right and proper they should do so. And to Madeline, who had lived for so long with a father who had put a gloss on his dreadful behaviour, and an uncle who had declared she was being 'looked after' when she was in fact being kept a prisoner, their honesty was refreshing.

'Wouldst'a like to see up yonder?' asked the woman, indicating the upstairs with a jerk of her head, having taken Madeline's measure and deciding she was to be trusted.

'Thank you, I would.'

The woman showed her over the cottage, which was leaky, draughty, cramped and damp, and Madeline saw why Philip wanted to rebuild it, and others of its like. With the Rochdale fortune there was a lot he could do to improve life for everyone; and it did not escape her notice that Philip was planning to use his money for the benefit of the estate, and not to waste it on drinking, gambling or womanizing as her father and uncle had done.

Madeline thanked the woman, and went outside. To her surprise she found that each of the other cottages had a woman standing outside it, arms folded over capacious bosoms, and she realized she must go into each cottage in turn so as not to slight anyone. She discovered a young couple in the first, who would benefit from improved conditions when their children were born; a man and his two children in the next and an elderly couple in the third, the bedridden old man having a definite twinkle in his eye. He spoke only the broadest dialect for the first few minutes, but when he saw that Madeline was not put out he gave a lusty laugh, saying 'Tha's all reet, lass. Tha's all reet,' making his wife, a very respectful woman, almost apoplectic!

Madeline laughed in return, and secured his undying devotion by calling him an old rogue.

Friendly relations having been established, he regaled her with tales of his youth, telling her that he had seen the cottages being built.

'And how do you feel about them being replaced?' asked Madeline, looking round the homely room and wondering whether he could bear to see it go.

'Eh, lass, I'll miss 'em and no mistake, but it's better so. It's the damp. Plays tricks on old bones.'

During the course of the conversation Madeline realized not only that the cottages were in need of rebuilding, but something else besides. She learned that Amelia and Percival's happy marriage was not a rarity. Because Old Ned and his wife, though they sparred good-naturedly throughout Madeline's entire visit, clearly enjoyed a happy married life as well. It was perplexing. Either she had by good fortune stumbled across the only two happily married couples in the country or else her mother's warnings had been sadly misplaced. But she was still not sure which it was.

After talking with Old Ned for a while longer, Madeline took her leave of him and his wife. As she did so she called over her shoulder mischievously, 'I'll just put wood in 'tole!'

Ned creased up in laughter, and his wife chuckled, and Madeline, feeling pleased to have made them laugh — and relieved that the strange phrase did indeed mean *close the door!* — went out to her waiting mare.

All in all, she felt, as she mounted the pretty little animal, her morning had been well spent; she was looking forward to discussing the plans again that evening with Philip now that she could visualize the scene and knew exactly what he meant to do.

But it was not long before her happy spirits evaporated. She had hardly left the cottages when she glimpsed movement out of the corner of her eye. She turned her head, but could see nothing. She searched the surrounding moors with her eyes but could not see any moving thing. Not a fox, not a hare, not a bird. Nothing. And yet something had caught her eye.

Feeling unsettled she set her mare to a brisk trot and headed towards the manor, turning her head to look behind her every few minutes, but still she could see nothing. But she felt sure she was being followed.

She quickened her horse's pace, beginning to feel anxious. She might not be able to see anything but she was becoming increasingly aware that, if danger threatened, she was far from help.

The manor now was coming into view. She set her mare to a faster pace still, and glanced over her shoulder once again. And this time she saw something. A man, far off, but following her.

She urged her mare onward, hoping that her lead would be long enough to allow her to reach the manor. But she was handicapped by the fact that she was riding sidesaddle, whilst her pursuer was riding astride.

The stables now came into view. She rode as fast as she could, scarcely daring to breathe, then let out a huge sigh of relief as she clattered into the stable yard. Safe at last!

Dismounting quickly she all but ran into the house.

'Where is the earl?' she demanded of Crump, who was at that moment crossing the hall.

'He's in his study, my lady, but . . . '

Madeline waited no longer, leaving Crump to say, 'he has someone with him,' to empty air.

'Philip, I have to speak to . . . ' said Madeline, throwing open the door to Philip's study, before belatedly realizing that the estate manager was with him.

'I can come back later,' said the manager, looking uncertainly from the earl to the countess and back again.

'Do that,' said Philip, his eyes never once leaving Madeline. 'Now then,' he said, when they were alone, standing up and coming round the desk to place his hands on his shoulders, 'tell me, what is the matter?'

'There was someone following me,' said Madeline, in her fear blurting the words out without preamble. 'Out on the moor. He has followed me all the way back to the manor.'

'Describe him,' said Philip curtly.

'I can't. He was too far away for me to see him properly. But a rough man, not a gentleman. He was dressed as a labourer. He was wearing some kind of breeches and a

193

shirt, but no coat. He must have something to do with Jack,' she said.

'No.' Philip shook his head.

'What then?' Madeline faltered, perplexed by Philip's attitude. He did not seem worried, or even surprised.

He sank back on to his desk with a frown. 'Madeline . . . '

'Yes?'

'You are not in any danger.'

'How can you say that? I have been followed across the moor. How can I not be in danger?'

'The man you saw . . . his name is Jenkins. He is someone who . . . works . . . for me from time to time.'

'He works for *you*?' asked Madeline, confused.

'Yes.'

'Then why was he following *me*?' She suddenly broke off, and backed away from him. 'You've been having me followed,' she said accusingly.

'Madeline — '

'Haven't you?' she demanded. All her fears rose up inside her, the legacy of her difficult past.

Why do I persist in thinking Philip is different? she asked herself. He is no better than my uncle.

A small voice inside her told her that he was nothing like her uncle, but she refused to listen to it. He had set a man to follow her, despite her express refusal to have a guard. It was unforgivable.

'Yes. I did,' he said.

'You admit it?' she demanded, her emotions churning.

He stood up and seized her by the shoulders. 'There are dangerous forces at work here, Madeline. You know that. You have seen them for yourself. Jack is involved in something extremely perilous, and the men who are pursuing him will stop at nothing,' he said fiercely. 'They will use any means in their power to bring him down, and if they feel it will be to their advantage to harm you then they will do so. I needed to know you would be safe.'

'So you set a man to spy on me?' she demanded.

'To protect you! Damn it, Madeline, why can't you see that? I don't want you to be in danger. I don't want you getting hurt.'

'No,' she returned angrily, 'I am far too valuable to you for that. Without me you cannot claim your inheritance. God forbid that anything should interfere with that.' The words were out before she could stop them.

Why had she said them? Why had she been

so unjust? she asked herself, wishing they could be recalled. But she knew why. It was because she could not bear to think of Philip caring about her, not when he was to marry Letitia. In some way she could not begin to understand, it hurt.

His mouth set into a grim line. 'You are my wife, Madeline, whether you like it or not,' he said, 'and as my wife you are under my care and protection. You may choose whatever form of protection you like, but you will not go anywhere without it. I will not allow any harm to come to you.' His voice became hard. 'As you yourself have pointed out, you are far too valuable for that. You will oblige me by letting me know when you have decided what form of protection you will accept, and I will provide it for you.' He was icily polite. 'Until then, I have a lot to do.'

It was a dismissal.

Madeline wrestled with herself. A part of her wanted to stay and argue, but she knew that it would do no good. Philip's face was implacable, and his mind was made up. And deep down, she did not want it to do any good. She knew there were dangers to be faced because of Philip's involvement with Jack, and a part of her was grateful to know that she was to be protected from them.

But another part of her was still haunted by

her past, and railed against the idea of being chaperoned for any reason whatsoever.

* * *

'Well?' asked Philip over dinner that night. 'Have you decided what form of protection you would like when you go out in future, Countess?'

He spoke with a stiff formality that was unlike his usual self, and Madeline found herself unaccountably longing for the friendship that had grown up between them over the preceding weeks to be restored. There was so much she wanted to talk to Philip about, but at the moment it was impossible.

A part of her still objected to the idea of being chaperoned every time she went out of the manor, but a part of her saw the sense of it. Since declaring that she would not be followed after Peters had attacked her she had often regretted her hasty words. Although a part of her was afraid of being followed, of being hemmed in and watched, another part of her recognized the danger inherent in being Philip's wife. She was, unwillingly, a part of a much larger drama; a drama that could perhaps even cost her her life.

She took a sip of wine, then dabbed her mouth with her napkin before laying it once more on her lap. 'I have,' she replied.

'And?'

'And . . . I have no objection to Jenkins accompanying me on my outings.'

She saw the hard lines at the corner of Philip's mouth soften.

'I don't want to have you followed,' he said gently, 'but it is necessary, and I'm glad you've agreed to it.'

'I was foolish to object,' said Madeline. Now that the subject had been brought out into the open she wanted to let him know how she felt. 'I know there is something happening here, something to do with Jack, and I know I might not be safe by myself. It's just that, when you first suggested I had someone with me when I went out, it reminded me too much of the way I was forced to live with my uncle.'

'I know. That is why I told Jenkins to be discreet,' said Philip.

'Has he been following me ever since the carriage accident?'

'Yes.'

'Then he has been discreet,' said Madeline appreciatively. 'This is the first time I have caught sight of him.'

'Jenkins knows his job,' Philip agreed.

Now that the air had been cleared between them, Madeline felt able to ask Philip about his trip to London to see Callaghan. 'Have you learnt any more about Jack from Callaghan?' she asked.

'Unfortunately not.' Philip took a drink of wine and put down his glass. 'Callaghan is giving nothing away. All I learnt was that he was pleased to get the message and even more pleased to get Peters. Other than that, he told me nothing. All he did was to give me his itinerary for the rest of the year. That way, if I need to contact him again, I will know where to find him.'

Madeline nodded.

Philip took a mouthful of beef and then said conversationally, 'You've seen the cottages, I hear.'

'Yes. It was when I was on my way back that I spotted Jenkins. It was he who told you I'd visited them, I suppose?'

'Actually, it wasn't. I've been talking to Old Ned.'

'You went up to the cottages as well today?'

'Yes. I wanted to inspect them with a view to my plans for their replacement. I went up after leaving you.' He cast her a humorous look. 'You've made quite a hit with Old Ned.'

Madeline smiled affectionately as she remembered the old rogue with a twinkle in his eye.

'You like him?' asked Philip curiously.

'Yes,' laughed Madeline. 'He's quite a character.'

For some reason, Philip recalled Letitia's description of Old Ned. 'That man's nothing but a dirty, disgraceful chur,' she'd said.

Why did he keep comparing Madeline to Letitia? he wondered, as Madeline gracefully rose from the table in order to leave him to his port. And why did he keep finding Letitia wanting? True, she was a hard and shallow woman, but she would make him a suitable countess. Wouldn't she?

And Madeline was far too young . . .

Unaware of his thoughts, Madeline left the room . . . and almost fell over one of the footmen, who was on his knees outside the door. Now what on earth was he doing there?

'Beg pardon, my lady,' said the footman, scrambling to his feet.

'That's all right . . . ?'

'Danson, my lady,' he said.

'That's all right, Danson.' She frowned slightly, as she wondered where she had heard the name before. Of course. Danson was the footman who had been paying Jenny too much attention. Still, he seemed polite enough now. And yet . . . and yet there was something about him she did not like.

For one disturbing moment the thought passed through her mind that he had been looking through the keyhole. A moment later she dismissed the idea, as she saw that he was clutching a button in his hand, and a glance at his coat showed her that one of his buttons was indeed missing from the front of it.

She smiled at herself. What a nonsensical thought! Footmen looking through keyholes, indeed. Really, she must not start imagining that everyone was watching her. It was too foolish! The poor man had simply lost his button, and bent down to reclaim it!

Besides, Jenny had not spoken of any further trouble with Danson, and it was probably as the maid had said: Danson was bored in the country, and had asked Jenny too many questions because he needed to find what interest he could in the lives of his fellow servants.

Making her way to the drawing-room, Madeline put the trivial incident out of her mind.

9

After weeks of preparation, the day of the ball finally arrived. Madeline was apprehensive as she checked her appearance in the cheval-glass. So far, no one had doubted the nature of her marriage to Philip, but his friends and neighbours would all be at the ball and she knew that she would have to play her part to perfection if she was to convince them that she and Philip were really married in the truest sense of the word. Although she did not like the idea of deceiving anyone, circumstances had forced her into a sham of a marriage, and she meant to see it through.

If it were not for her apprehension she would have enjoyed the afternoon. She had been delightfully pampered. After bathing in scented water, Jenny had helped her to dress in her most beautiful ball gown. It was a shining example of the modiste's art, and was a credit to Miss Silverstone. The gauze overskirt, which was as light as gossamer, split beneath her breasts to reveal an underskirt of oyster pink, its satin gleaming in the evening sunlight. The delicate sleeves, short and becomingly puffed, were decorated with the lightest frostwork, and the same frostwork was repeated round the underskirt's hem. Her hair, too, was a miracle. Monsieur LeTour, the fashionable *friseur*, had travelled over from York especially to do her hair — Madeline had protested that Jenny dressed her hair beautifully, but Philip had insisted, and Jenny had been just as eager for the great man to do it. 'For I'll learn a thing or two, I've no doubt,' she had said to Madeline.

Madeline's fair hair had been piled on top of her head and then caught up with a silver comb. Glossy ringlets had been teased out to frame her face and to fall over one shoulder, and she knew she had never looked better.

Round her throat she wore a pearl necklace.

'You look lovely, my lady,' said Jenny mistily.

'Wish me luck,' said Madeline as she pulled on her long evening-gloves; then, summoning her courage, she went out on to the landing.

Reaching the top of the stairs she saw Philip standing at the bottoms of the stairs, looking magnificent. It was the first time she had ever seen him in evening-dress. He was wearing a dark blue tail-coat with a figured waistcoat and a pair of skin-tight pantaloons, which showed off his lean and rangy body to great advantage. Snowy linen could be seen at his neck and at his wrists. A diamond tiepin caught a ray of evening sunshine and winked in his cravat.

At that moment he looked up and saw her.

His eyes flashed, and Madeline felt suddenly breathless.

Forcing herself to go forward she walked along the landing and began to descend the stairs. She felt Philip's eyes on her with every step she took. She saw his gaze rove over her oyster-pink gown and a moment later he was striding up the stairs to meet her, taking them two at a time. He met her on the half-landing, his eyes running over her beautifully arranged hair, her sparkling eyes and her moist lips, and the intensity of his look made her heart begin to beat more quickly.

'You look beautiful,' he said. The huskiness of his voice told her that it was no empty compliment. 'Come.'

He gave her his arm and together they went down the last few stairs.

To Madeline's surprise he led her into his study.

'Should we not be ready to greet our guests?' she asked.

'This will only take a moment,' he said.

He took her over to the gilded looking-glass and turned her gently so that she was facing it. Then he started to undo the clasp on her pearls. In her surprise she put up a hand to stop him. But as her fingers touched his a bolt of electricity shot through her, and she dropped her hand as though scalded.

She saw his eyes flare. But then he continued to remove her pearls. He lifted something from the table behind him; there was a flash of fire; and then he placed another necklace round her throat.

'The Rochdale diamonds,' he said.

Madeline gasped. The necklace was fabulous. 'But I can't . . . '

'Why not?' he asked. 'You are the Countess of Pemberton, Madeline. It's only right you should wear the Rochdale diamonds. And for your ears,' he said. He turned her round and he gave her the matching earrings, deftly helping her to arrange them.

He placed his hands on her shoulders and for a moment she thought he was going to kiss her on the lips. But then a carriage crunched on the gravel outside and he kissed her lightly on the forehead instead. Even that slight touch was enough to intensify all her confusing and perplexing feelings, and she was glad that the ball was upon them. At least in company there could be no more disturbingly intimate moments; moments she dared not admit were becoming increasingly precious to her. Because if she admitted it, what then? Philip was destined for Letitia, and she would do well not to forget it.

Jason Fellows was the first guest to arrive. He often made the trip to Yorkshire as his mother's family was from that part of the country and his maternal grandparents still lived there.

'My dear Philip!' he said, warmly taking Philip by the hand. 'And Lady Pemberton. You look exquisite.' He made Madeline a low bow, and then dispensed with formality to say good-humouredly, 'Don't tell me I'm the first to arrive?'

'Someone has to be,' Madeline consoled him.

'Very true. And perhaps it is just as well. I've a mind to find a wife and settle down myself, so I need to get an early start! You see what you have begun!' he said to Philip with a laugh.

'There will be plenty of young ladies here tonight — all willing to talk about music and art!' Philip spoke gravely, but a quirk at the corner of his mouth gave him away.

'I'm sure there will be,' said Jason, knowing that Philip was deliberately reminding him of the conversation they had had about marriageable young ladies in London. 'The only trouble is, I don't know the first thing about music and art myself!'

Another party had by this time arrived and Jason moved through into the ballroom, leaving Madeline and Philip to greet their other guests. Lord and Lady Cadogan were followed by Mr and Mrs Frobisher, The Honourable Mrs Diddington and five of her daughters, all of whom were eager to meet the new countess.

And then Philip's cousin, Stuart Letts, arrived.

'Stuart. So glad you could join us,' murmured Philip.

Madeline, standing next to him, realized that he was not pleased to see his cousin, whatever his words. But she had no time to wonder about it, as Stuart moved on and more guests claimed her attention. Soon the house was ringing with the sound of music as the orchestra struck up the chords of the first dance.

'Come,' said Philip, taking Madeline's arm. 'The guests are all here. Now it is time for us to open the ball.'

Madeline had always loved to dance, but had had little opportunity to do so — until now.

She took her place at the top of the set, Philip facing her, and swept him an elegant curtsy. And then the dance began. Madeline could not remember ever having enjoyed herself so much. Her nerves completely vanished and she remembered all of the complicated steps; steps she had practised with her mother in snatched moments of happiness, when her father had been away from home.

'Oh! My dear Countess! Isn't this wonderful?!' gasped Clarissa an hour later, when Philip and Madeline were mingling with their guests. 'I've never enjoyed myself so much in my life. I do declare I've danced every dance! And Amelia is having a wonderful time as well. So good of you to invite her and Percival along this evening. They are having a marvellous time!'

'It was a pleasure.' Madeline glanced at the happy couple, who were dancing at the other side of the room.

They were interrupted by Jason. 'Miss Rogers. May I have the honour of your hand for the next dance?' he asked, coming up to the two ladies.

As soon as Clarissa had accepted Jason's hand for the next dance, Madeline found her own hand being sought. 'My dear Countess, may I have the honour of this dance?'

'Mr Letts,' said Madeline, turning to see Philip's cousin.

'Please. We are related now. Will you not call me Stuart?'

'Stuart. I would be delighted.'

The ballroom was looking entrancing, Madeline noted, as Stuart led her out on to the floor in preparation for a cotillion. All the effort she and Mrs Potts had put in had been worth it. The chandeliers sparkled and shone, the mirrors gleamed, and the green-and-white chairs blended beautifully with the flowers that had been brought in from the gardens, and which now filled huge vases all around the house.

'May I say how lovely you're looking tonight, Countess?' Stuart asked.

Madeline was still not used to the compliments which prevailed at social gatherings, but she managed to reply lightly, 'Thank you.'

'Philip is a lucky man.'

There was a suggestive expression on his face as he said it, as though there was more to the commonplace remark than there appeared to be, and Madeline decided to change the subject.

'What brings you to Yorkshire?' she asked, turning the conversation into less personal channels. 'Some kind of business, I think you said?'

'Oh, nothing of any importance,' he replied

vaguely. 'Just a little property that needs attending to from time to time.'

His conversation was light and agreeable and, but for the fact he paid her rather too many compliments, she was happy to dance with him, and happy to accept his hand for a second time later in the evening, this time for a quadrille.

'Quite the gentleman, isn't he, Mr Letts?' giggled the youngest Miss Diddington as she collapsed into a chair beside Madeline once the quadrille was over. 'I was hoping he'd ask me for a waltz, but Mama says I am not allowed to dance it even if there is one.'

'You are perhaps a little young for the waltz,' said Madeline.

'Oh, pooh! That's what Mama says. Oh, look, here is the earl come to claim you. When I am a married woman I shall waltz until my shoes drop off!'

'Was Miss Diddington being entertaining?' asked Philip as he claimed Madeline's hand.

Madeline laughed. 'She tells me that when she is a married woman she is going to waltz until her shoes fall off!'

'A waltz. I should have thought of that,' said Philip meditatively as he looked down into Madeline's eyes.

'I don't know how to waltz,' she admitted as they approached the floor.

'Don't you, indeed?' There was a strange glow in his eyes. 'Then I must teach you. But not here. Somewhere more private, I think.'

Taking her by the hand, he led her out of the ballroom, across the hall and into the library — the one room not being used that evening. The sound of the music and chatter faded away behind them.

'Philip! We can't leave our guests!' she said as he closed the door.

'They'll manage very well without us for a few minutes.' He smiled down at her. 'Come. I'm not going to eat you,' he teased.

A highly improper image flashed into her innocent mind, an image that centred around the kisses he had bestowed on her, but fortunately he was not privy to her thoughts.

'First, I place my hand on your waist, so.'

He suited the action to the word, and Madeline felt a surge of heat where his hand rested.

'Then you place your hand on my shoulder.'

She lifted her hand hesitantly and rested it on his shoulder. Through the cloth of his tail-coat she felt the hard ridge of his muscles and her fingers unconsciously ran over them, taking pleasure from their strength.

'And then I take your other hand.'

Even through her evening-glove she could

feel the heat of his touch. 'Now what happens?' she asked, her voice low.

'Now you trust yourself to me.'

He took a step to the side and, with his arm guiding her, she felt her feet follow his. She soon picked up the steps of the dance and began to follow more easily. They glided round the room, avoiding tables and chairs as though they did not exist. Their bodies were not touching except where their hands met, or where Philip's hand rested on her slender waist, but the distance between them was slowly shrinking. Philip's hands slid downwards, pressing her against him, and her arms slipped round his neck. His head lowered and — a knock came at the door.

'Damn!' said Philip, stepping away from Madeline just in time as Crump, the butler, entered the room.

'Begging you pardon, my lord.' Crump was blissfully unaware that he had interrupted anything. 'Young Cedric Neith has taken more wine than is good for him and I fear he may insult some of the ladies. I have tried to reason with him, but to no avail. I hesitated to call the footmen, my lord, for fear that, if pushed, he may start a brawl.'

'Damn the puppy!' said Philip. 'Can his father not keep him in line?'

Crump's face spoke volumes: young Mr

Neith's father was completely ineffectual.

'All right, Crump. I'll come at once.' He turned to Madeline. 'I'm sorry, I . . . '

'I understand.' Madeline swallowed her disappointment. 'In any case, it is time I returned to our guests.'

Philip made her a bow and then strode out of the room, Crump following behind.

Madeline gave herself a minute or two to recover. Her pulse was still fluttering and she walked over to the window to get some air. Outside, the night was cloudless. Silver stars winked and glittered in the velvet sky.

Now you trust yourself to me. Philip's words rang in her ears. He had been talking about the dance, but his words had gone far deeper than that, because she realized she *had* trusted herself to him. She had never thought she would trust any man but, impossible as it seemed, she trusted Philip. Utterly and completely.

But then she reminded herself that she could only trust him because they were not truly married. If they were really married . . . if they were really married, what then?

It was useless to think about it. They were not really married, and they never would be. That thought, instead of filling her with relief, gave her pain.

She shook her head. It was nonsensical.

How could it give her pain?

She did not know. But it did.

She turned away from the window. It was time for her to return to her guests. She had already been away too long.

Going back into the ballroom she was soon accosted by Stuart.

'Madeline! I've been looking everywhere for you!' he exclaimed. 'I want to claim your hand for the next dance.'

'I've already danced with you twice,' Madeline reminded him.

'And why shouldn't you make it three? You're a married woman, not a young girl, after all.'

'There are other young ladies . . . '

'They have all found partners.'

He was looking at her so hopefully that at last she relented. 'Very well.'

He beamed in reply and offered her his arm.

'But this must be the last time,' she said.

10

'Not again!' Madeline exclaimed involuntarily as, looking up from her escritoire, she saw Stuart riding up to the house. In the week since the ball he had visited the manor three times, and this was his fourth. It was not that she did not like him. He was amusing company and a good conversationalist. But he paid her too many compliments, he held on to her hand rather too long when he kissed it, and he made her feel generally ill at ease.

'Not again?' asked Philip from the doorway.

Madeline turned with a start. She had not heard him enter the drawing-room.

She flushed slightly; she did not want Philip to think that she did not welcome his cousin, or indeed any of his friends and relatives. It was just that there seemed to be something so particular about Stuart's attentions. Although she was probably imagining it, she told herself. Being unused to society she did not know how dapper young gentlemen usually behaved.

'Who is it this time?' asked Philip, walking

into the room. 'Clarissa?'

'Not at all,' said Madeline. 'I'm always pleased to see Clarissa.'

'Then who . . . ?' Philip began as he walked over to the window, then saw who it was for himself. 'Ah. Stuart,' he said.

Madeline saw him tense. Philip was a hospitable host, but Stuart had taken to visiting the manor on some pretext or other almost every day, and staying for hours when he called. He had a lot of time on his hands, no doubt, but his behaviour was thoughtless none the less.

'Don't worry,' he said. 'I'll take him into the study. I know you have a lot to do.'

In fact, the ball being over, Madeline had much less to do than previously, but she suspected that Philip wanted a quiet word with his cousin, and guessed he was going to suggest, tactfully, that Stuart should give them some warning of his visits in future rather than just turning up unexpectedly every other day. So she did not remonstrate, and settled herself to writing her letters: one to Lady Weatherby, and the other to Emma, telling her all about the ball.

Outside in the hall, Philip met Stuart and greeted him warmly. Then he suggested they retire to his study.

'Oh!' Stuart looked put out. 'Madeline not

216

at home? I just thought I'd call to pay my respects.'

'Later.' Philip was polite but firm.

Stuart was about to protest when he changed his mind. Philip might be smiling but the smile was predatory and the younger man raised his hand to his neck, nervously loosening his cravat before he accepted Philip's invitation to join him in the study. If the truth be told he was sadly put out, as he had not expected to find Philip at home.

'Now,' said Philip, sitting on the edge of his desk and folding his arms across his chest as Stuart settled himself in a Hepplewhite chair, 'I think you'd better tell me what this is all about.'

Stuart looked surprised. 'I'm not sure I know what you mean.'

'Paying court to Lady Pemberton. That's what I mean.'

'Paying court? That's a strange way of putting it,' said Stuart with a nervous smile.

'Dancing with her three times at the ball. Coming to the house nearly every day on some pretext or other and then paying her the most marked attention. Telling her her eyes are as deep as forest pools and her lips are as pink as a rose. And yes, I heard that,' he said as he saw Stuart's startled expression. 'If you want to pay extravagant compliments to married ladies I suggest you make sure their husbands are not within hearing distance first.'

'If I didn't know better I'd think you were jealous,' Stuart remarked, with a clumsy attempt at humour.

'Don't be ridiculous.' But even as he said it Philip had a flash of self-knowledge, and no matter how ridiculous it seemed he realized that he *was* jealous. The thought of Madeline being courted by Stuart made his blood boil. He had watched his cousin's clumsy attempts to win Madeline's favour with distaste, a distaste made all the stronger by seeing Madeline's obvious embarrassment, but he had told himself that what he felt was not jealousy, it was concern for Madeline's happiness. But he could no longer deny it. It was the green-eyed monster. To have her monopolized by Fitzgrey had been bad enough, but to have her pursued by Stuart, of all people. A young puppy without any of the qualities she needed to make her happy. He ignored the fact that, had Stuart possessed every virtue, he would have felt just the same.

'I agree,' said Stuart. 'It is ridiculous. After all, why should you feel jealous when Madeline is not your wife?'

'What?' Philip fixed a penetrating glance on Stuart and pushed himself away from the

218

desk until he stood towering over the young man. 'What do you mean, Madeline is not my wife?'

'Oh, you've no need to worry,' said Stuart evenly, but pressing himself against the back of his chair none the less: Philip when roused was a magnificent sight, and not one he had any wish to experience at closer quarters. 'Your secret's safe with me.'

'What are you talking about?' demanded Philip.

'You and Madeline. You're not married at all — at least not in any real sense of the word. Your marriage is a sham to get round your father's will. You see, I know all about it.'

Philip's glance was hard. 'Indeed.'

Stuart quaked as he looked at Philip's grim face but then he recovered his nerve and continued. 'Yes. Indeed. You see, Aunt Honoria told me everything. She said — '

'Ah! Aunt Honoria.' Philip's mouth set in a line. 'I suspected she was behind it.'

'It was Aunt Honoria who told me the marriage was a masquerade, designed to let you collect your fortune, if that's what you mean,' said Stuart. 'I can't say I blame you, and neither does she. There's a lot of money at stake, and it would be stupid to let it go to waste.'

'I don't know what Aunt Honoria told

you,' said Philip, 'but whatever it was, I suggest you forget it. Madeline and I are man and wife, and — '

'Oh, no, that won't wash,' said Stuart, pursing his lips and shaking his head. 'You see, I saw the letter.'

'Letter?' Philip demanded. 'What letter?'

'The letter you wrote to Aunt Honoria before you went to visit her, telling her all about it. How you wanted to marry Letitia, but if you did so you'd have to forfeit the fortune. How Mr Murgo'd come up with the idea of your making a temporary marriage, and how you'd married Madeline in order to inherit the fortune. And how, at the end of six months — once you'd got your hands on the money –– you intended to have the marriage annulled and marry Letitia.'

Philip sat back on his desk. 'She showed you the letter. I never expected that.' His eyes became hard again. 'But that doesn't mean you can come here making love to Madeline. What I do is my business; what Madeline does is hers. It has nothing to do with you.'

'Oh, but it does. You see, I intend to marry Madeline — once your six months is up.'

'You *what?*' Philip stood up, towering over his cousin once more.

Stuart almost stood up himself, but he had the sudden alarming feeling that if he did that, Philip might knock him down. Instead he remained seated. 'Really, Philip,' he said, his voice holding a peevish edge, 'it's not like you to play dog in the manger. You don't want Madeline, but you're determined I shouldn't have her either. I can't for the life of me see why.'

'Aunt Honoria has a lot to answer for,' said Philip between gritted teeth. 'What the devil did she mean by it?'

'Come, come, Philip. That's obvious enough. She was trying to help.'

'Help! Aunt Honoria doesn't want to help. She wants to make mischief.'

'No.' Stuart shook his head. 'There you're wrong. She's worried about Madeline. She told me so herself. Once the marriage is annulled Madeline will have nothing left.'

'She'll have a handsome house and an even handsomer annuity,' said Philip, his eyes flaring.

'But that won't do for a woman as young as Madeline. She'll want a husband. A proper home. Children. A life.'

'By God, you're asking for trouble,' said Philip, surprising Stuart as well as himself by the strength of his feelings. 'You come into my house, make love to my wife, and then proceed to lecture me on Madeline's future.'

'And why shouldn't she have a future?'

demanded Stuart. 'And why shouldn't that future be with me? I'm young. Personable. With no nasty habits. I'm rich enough, good looking enough. And Madeline likes me.'

'Oh does she?' Philip's voice was threatening.

'Yes. She's always pleasant to me when I come here.'

'Madeline is a lady,' said Philip icily. 'She's pleasant to everyone.'

'Maybe that's so,' retorted Stuart. 'But she's getting used to me. And in a few short months, when your marriage is annulled, why shouldn't she start to think of me as a husband?'

'You can say this, sitting here, in my house, about my wife?' demanded Philip.

'I can say it, sitting here, in your house, about your *pretend* wife,' returned Stuart. 'If you loved her I wouldn't dream of saying these things and you know it. Besides, if you loved her, there wouldn't be any point. But that isn't the case. What is the case is that Madeline will soon need a husband, and I am in need of a wife. She is young, beautiful, intelligent — and when you have made your handsome settlement on her she will also be rich — '

'And now you have said enough. I will not abandon Madeline to a fortune-hunter. I want you out of this house right now.' He pulled the bell. 'Ah, Crump,' he said when the butler answered the bell. 'Mr Letts is leaving. Be so good as to show him out.'

Stuart gave him a glowering look but he had no choice. With a last angry glare at Philip he left the room.

And why did I behave like that? Philip asked himself as he strode over to the window. Stuart didn't say anything that wasn't true. And as for me accusing him of being a fortune-hunter, he's nothing of the kind. And what's more, I know it.

But he knew why he had behaved like that. Underneath, he knew. And what's more, he had known for some time. It was simply that he hadn't wanted to admit it. But now he could deny it no longer.

He was in love with Madeline.

Yes. He was in love with her.

As he thought over the time they had spent together he realized he loved everything about her: her delectable curves; her elfin face; the way tiny hairs escaped from her chignon at the base of her neck, tempting him to kiss her soft white skin.

And more. So much more.

Her physical beauty, her innocently tantalizing mannerisms, were a part of what he felt for her, but they were nowhere near the

223

whole. Her courage and her resilience, her optimism and her determination — if her beauty aroused his admiration, it was these qualities that aroused his respect. And the depth and the complexity of her character; these were the things that bound him to her.

Such depth he had not expected to come across in one so young, nor in a woman, no matter what her age. Most women led such sheltered lives they had no need of depth or complexity, courage or resilience, intelligence or understanding; but Madeline's life had been difficult, and had taught her lessons that the vapid and insipid young misses who irritated him would never learn. And yet all these qualities were wrapped up with gentler features: a sense of humour that, despite the hardness of her early life, bubbled just beneath the surface; a consideration for others that had been evident on her visits to see the tenants, and an enjoyment of life that her early years had not been able to crush.

Yes, he was in love with her, no matter how young she might be. And what a fool he had been for not seeing it before.

But Letitia . . .

What a coil it was. He had been wrong to think he could marry Letitia, and yet it would not be the act of a gentleman to draw back now. But how could he not draw back? He couldn't possibly marry Letitia now that he knew he loved Madeline.

He shook his head. Although he knew that it was a problem that would have to be faced sooner or later, just for the moment he did not want to think of it.

But even if the problem of Letitia was solved, he knew there were other problems facing him. Although he had realized he was in love with Madeline, he did not know what her feelings were for him.

She was afraid of marriage, that much he had discovered. To begin with, he had thought she was simply afraid of men, and had thought that was a natural result of having been Gareth Delaware's ward. But he had come to realize it was more than that; she was afraid of marriage itself. But why? That was the question he could not answer.

What had her parents' marriage been like? he wondered. Had it been warm and loving, as the marriage of his own parents had been? Or had it been cold and hard? He had no way of knowing. But what he did know was that he must show her just how fulfilling and rewarding a marriage could be if he was going to have a chance to win her hand, not just as a temporary arrangement, but for ever. And here he had an advantage: time and circumstances were on his side. He was already married to Madeline, at least in name, and he knew that she had begun to enjoy herself as his wife. He had seen her start to relax in his company, despite the fact that they often crossed swords, and he had watched her bloom and blossom into a confident young woman.

And then he thought of the other sides of marriage. He knew that she had physical feelings for him, although he suspected that she herself did not yet understand them. She had led a knowing life in some ways, being exposed to her uncle's crude and leering cronies, but in the matter of fulfilling physical feelings between a man and a woman she was a complete innocent. But he wanted her to experience them, and he wanted her to experience them with him.

He had a little over four months in which to teach her that marriage was to be enjoyed rather than feared, he realized.

He meant to make the most of them.

11

'At last!' Philip smiled, then gave the letter he had been reading to Madeline. 'Emma is over her cold. She will be here at the end of next week.'

Madeline picked up the letter and read it with pleasure. It seemed she was finally going to meet her sister-in-law.

She had had some qualms about imposing on Emma's credibility, but Philip had seemed unconcerned. He had told her that she was not deceiving anyone: that she really was his wife; that she was in fact Emma's sister-in-law, and therefore need have no guilty conscience about being introduced as such.

At last Madeline had come to see it from Philip's point of view. She was indeed the Countess of Pemberton, and as she did not want Emma to be burdened with a true account of their marriage, she felt it was better to do as Philip suggested, allowing Emma to enjoy meeting her new sister-in-law.

And Madeline was concerned that Emma *should* enjoy herself. She wanted to make sure that Emma's time in Yorkshire was happy. Indeed, if she had really been Philip's wife, his true wife, she would have suggested that Emma should come and live with them. But as she herself was only to be the mistress of the manor until the end of December she could make no such suggestion, much as she would have liked to do so.

She was just about to hand the letter back to Philip when she heard a carriage drawing up in front of the manor. She was surprised, as she was not expecting anyone. But perhaps it was Clarissa. Handing Philip the letter she went to the window to see who their guest might be. The carriage came to a halt, the door opened, the step was let down . . . and out of it came Letitia Bligh. As Madeline watched, Letitia straightened up. The elegant young woman regarded the manor with a proprietorial air before opening her fashionable parasol. Then, sheltering her flawless complexion from the summer sun, she walked up to the front door.

Following her at a distance of some five or six paces was her mousy companion.

Madeline froze. She did not know why, but for some reason she had not expected to see Letitia at the manor. And yet why not? Letitia had every right to be there; more right, if truth be told, than Madeline herself.

In another minute the door opened and Crump announced, 'Miss Bligh.'

Letitia was the epitome of fashionable elegance as she swept into the room, her willowy figure displaying her silk carriage-dress with its exquisite lace trimmings to great advantage.

'Philip!' Letitia greeted Philip in beautifully modulated tones. She crossed the room towards him — completely ignoring Madeline — and took his arm, kissing him on the cheek. 'I am just on my way to stay with friends in Scotland, and as the carriage had to pass so close by the manor I could not resist the idea of calling to see you on the way.'

'Letitia.' Philip returned her greeting.

'And Madeline,' said Letitia, at last deigning to notice Madeline. 'It is delightful to see you again.' She put her free hand firmly on Philip's arm as she spoke and smiled at Madeline with a tigress's smile — making sure, however, that Philip did not see it.

Madeline greeted Letitia coolly.

Philip invited Letitia to sit down, but she looked out of the window and said, 'It is such a pleasant day, and I have been sitting for so long in the carriage. Can we not take a stroll?'

'If you wish,' he replied.

Taking a stroll with Letitia and Philip, watching them laughing and talking together was, for some reason, the last thing Madeline wanted to do, but for the sake of politeness it could not be avoided.

As they left the manor Philip offered one arm to Madeline and the other to Letitia, leaving Letitia's companion to trail along behind. It was not an arrangement Madeline liked, but nevertheless it must be endured.

'And how are you enjoying your time at the manor?' Letitia asked Madeline, as they strolled along the gravel paths that surrounded the manor.

'I am enjoying it very well,' said Madeline, feeling ill at ease. Letitia was somehow managing to remind her of the temporary nature of her marriage to Philip by talking of *your time* at the manor, whilst seeming to be doing nothing more than making polite conversation.

'And Emma is soon to join you, I understand,' Letitia continued. 'How tiresome you will find it, having a young girl dogging your footsteps and demanding to be taken out and about. You must be firm with her, and make her realize you will stand no nonsense.'

'I don't believe I will find it tiresome,' remarked Madeline. She was looking forward to the young girl's visit, having heard a great deal about her from Philip, and hoped to make her feel at home.

'Really?' Letitia laughed. 'I think you will

be surprised. Girls of that age think of nothing but parties and expect their elders and betters to escort them to every provincial amusement, no matter how inconvenient it may be. They should be kept in the nursery, in my opinion, like the children they really are, and not let out until they are of marriageable age. Do you not think so, Philip?' she asked, turning her face up to his.

'If you say so,' he replied.

Letitia seemed satisfied with his reply, but to Madeline it had seemed wooden. Letitia and Philip had different ideas where Emma — and any other children — were concerned, it seemed.

Still, it was nothing to do with her. And so she firmly reminded herself.

Letitia, clearly feeling that she had wasted enough time on Madeline, turned her attention to Philip and started regaling him with stories about people who, though known to Letitia and Philip, were completely unknown to Madeline.

They walked as far as the ha-ha, a clever contrivance which took the form of a deep ditch separating the lawns from the park beyond. The ha-ha ensured that the sheep and deer which grazed in the park did not invade the gardens and eat the carefully cultivated plants. It was so much better than a wall or fence, thought Madeline appreciatively, as, excluded from the conversation, she turned her attention to the landscape. A wall or fence would obscure the view, but the ha-ha allowed the view to continue uninterrupted for as far as the eye could see.

'Oh, my! It's so lovely here!' said Letitia's timid companion, who had caught up with them now that they had stopped for a few minutes.

'Have you been to Yorkshire before?' asked Madeline kindly, engaging the elderly lady in conversation.

'Oh, yes!' she said, going pink and looking flustered at being spoken to so politely by a countess. 'But it is not all as pretty as this!'

When they again walked on, Madeline took the opportunity of pointing out the various views to Letitia's companion, and in this way she gave herself a reason to let go of Philip's arm and walk ahead with the elderly spinster. Slowly but surely, Letitia and Philip dropped further and further behind them. Madeline was glad. She was not comfortable in their company, and as she could not very well go back to the house without seeming rude, this was the best solution. It spared her from being a third party in their conversation whilst preserving the niceties.

Unbeknownst to her, Philip, behind her,

was not absorbed in Letitia's conversation as she supposed, but was instead absorbed in her. She looked very becoming in her layered white muslin gown, he thought, with her blue satin slippers and a blue ribbon threaded through her hair.

' . . . the Regent has always had a soft spot for him, but if he is not careful, Brummell will one day overstep the mark — you're not listening to me, Philip,' said Letitia, realizing that it was so.

'Hm? I'm sorry, Letitia. You were saying?'

'I was saying that Brummell has been getting careless recently, and has made one or two remarks that the Regent has not quite liked. But you are not interested in Brummell's latest *mots*, *bon* or otherwise. And it's easy to see why.' Letitia glanced at Madeline.

'Letitia,' he began. He had been wanting to speak to her about their future, or lack of it, ever since he had realized he was in love with Madeline, but as she had been travelling he had not had an opportunity to do so. Her visit, however, had provided him with the chance he had needed, and now that her flow of conversation had come to an end he knew he must speak.

To his surprise, however, before he could say any more, Letitia held up her hand.

'Don't tell me.' She gave a bright smile. 'Let me guess.'

Philip was so surprised that he said nothing.

With perfect good humour Letitia said, 'You are distracted because you have realized you can't go ahead and marry me. You have fallen in love with Madeline, and you find that a marriage of convenience with me is no longer what you want. But you are too much of a gentleman to feel comfortable about going back on our agreement, even though it was not binding on either of us — which, as I recall, was my doing and not yours.'

Philip looked at her in amazement. 'How did you know?' he asked.

She smiled winningly. 'It is obvious. At least, it is obvious to someone who knows you as well as I do.'

He looked at her curiously. 'And do you not mind?' He was surprised as he took in her clear eyes and her understanding smile. 'I know how much you wanted to be a countess, Letitia. I thought you would be angry, and yet you seem to be taking it very well.'

She gave a shrug of her elegant shoulders. 'What other way is there to take it? There was never any formal agreement between us and besides, you are already married to Madeline.

I can't *force* you to annul the marriage. If I created a scene it would make no difference; it wouldn't change anything. You would still be Madeline's husband and she would still be your wife. And so I wish you happy.' She looked ahead to Madeline. 'She is a delightful young woman. You have made a good choice.'

Philip's eyes, too, went to Madeline. In doing so they missed the gleam of pure hatred that darted suddenly from Letitia's eye.

'Yes. I have made a good choice,' he said softly. 'And it is generous of you to admit it.'

Letitia's features were once more perfectly schooled as Philip turned to face her again. 'I hope that we may still be friends,' she said with a show of frankness. 'We will have to meet each other at social gatherings and I would not like there to be any awkwardness between us. I wish you well, Philip, and hope you will wish me the same.'

He nodded. 'I do.'

'Then let us go and join the others. They will be beginning to wonder where we are.'

She took his arm and, walking more briskly, they soon caught up with Madeline and Miss Wilkes.

'This has been a perfect break in our journey,' said Letitia. 'It is so good to see friends. But now I believe we must be going

— we are to dine with the Armitages this evening and if we don't leave soon we will be late.'

They made their farewells, and before long Letitia's carriage was once more on its way.

'Did you enjoy yourself with Miss Wilkes?' asked Philip genially as he went back inside with Madeline.

'She was very pleasant,' said Madeline politely.

'Good.'

'And — did you enjoy your time with Miss Bligh?' she asked nonchalantly.

'Yes. Very much.'

'Oh.'

Her voice held a hint of dejection.

Just for a moment he wondered whether he should tell her that his understanding with Letitia was at an end but then he decided against it. If he told her that he no longer wanted to marry Letitia then, given her fear of marriage, she would feel vulnerable and might be afraid of becoming trapped. He wanted her to love him as much as he loved her before revealing to her the true nature of his feelings for her. When that time came he would tell her his arrangement with Letitia was over, and not before.

★ ★ ★

236

Madeline looked around Emma's room, making sure that everything was ready. A vase of fresh flowers stood on the dressing-table, the windows were open, letting in the balmy breeze, and the room was freshly cleaned and polished. All it needed now was its occupant. And she should be arriving at any time.

Madeline was in the garden when Emma finally arrived. As the young girl stepped out of the carriage Madeline caught her first glimpse of her sister-in-law.

How good it would have been to welcome Emma to the house if she had really been its mistress, its permanent mistress, she thought. Having no family herself, Madeline was glad to find herself with a sister, even if it was only for a few months, and went lightly down the steps to welcome Emma.

Emma was a slight girl of sixteen years old; a schoolgirl, but one who was just emerging from that phase of life. Her figure was slim and delicate as yet, but it was just beginning to show signs of curves. Even so, Madeline could quickly see why she had found Emma's dresses so tight and uncomfortable when she had borrowed them for a while in London!

As well as a slight figure, Emma had a good-humoured countenance and a pretty face, with dark hair tousled by the journey and bright amber eyes. Her features were not as harsh as Philip's, but still bore the unmistakable Rochdale stamp.

'Emma!' Madeline greeted the young girl with open arms.

'Madeline! How lovely to meet you at last! Oh, I knew I should like you, and so I do! I have been telling Philip we would get along all the way from the inn. And was it not good of the Greys to bring me so far, for I'm sure it was out of their way!'

Emma had been brought as far as the neighbouring town by her friendly Bath neighbours, the Greys, who had been going to visit relatives in the Lake District. They had been delighted to bring the young girl most of the way in their carriage, and she had then been collected by Philip from the nearest inn.

'It was very kind of them,' said Madeline, as she gave Emma a hug.

Much of Madeline's reserve had left her since meeting Philip, and it now seemed natural to her to greet a new acquaintance, especially one she knew so much about, with open arms, instead of with hesitancy and suspicion.

'Your room's all ready for you,' said Madeline as she and Emma went into the house, closely followed by Philip. 'Would you like to rest after your journey?'

'I am tired of resting,' said Emma.

'You're looking a little pale,' said Philip protectively, as he took in Emma's countenance with a brotherly eye.

'Only because I have been cooped up inside for the past two weeks with a cold, when really I only needed to be cooped up for two days.' She turned to Madeline. 'Everyone is so used to me being delicate they *will* fuss over me, and Philip is the same.' Her sweet smile took any rancour out of her words, and Madeline found herself sympathizing with the girl.

'Sometimes too much attention can be as bad as not enough,' she agreed.

'You understand,' cried Emma. She turned to Philip mischievously. 'You see, I told you she would!'

Philip laughed. 'You, miss, are well on the way to becoming a minx. However, if you promise to tell me if ever you feel unwell, I promise not to fuss over you. You can ride in the grounds and swim in the river to your heart's content.'

Emma gave him an impulsive kiss and they all moved into the drawing-room.

Madeline rang for tea, and whilst they drank and ate, Emma regaled them with an account of her journey and her plans for her visit. Apart from going to see everyone she knew on the estate she was longing to go riding over the moors, and to climb her favourite trees — as well as hoping that Madeline would take her round the fashionable shops in York. She was half-way between a girl and a woman, and her interests — riding and tree-climbing on the one hand, and shopping and novels on the other — reflected the transition.

After an enjoyable tea the three of them took a stroll in the grounds, with Philip giving one arm to Madeline and the other to Emma, before returning to the house. Emma, tired after her journey and her exciting day, bid Madeline and Philip a good night, whereupon Madeline and Philip repaired to the drawing-room and companionably discussed the day's events.

'How delicate is Emma?' asked Madeline, concerned to know as much as she could about her sister-in-law.

Philip thought. 'As a child she always had something wrong with her: mumps, measles, coughs, colds and sore throats. Everything a child can have, Emma had.'

'And now?'

Philip thought. 'She still has the odd complaint, but I think there is something in what she says — she does tend to be fussed over. If she had not had so many childhood illnesses I would not now think of her as delicate. Why do you ask?'

'I just wondered whether I ought to be encouraging her to be active over the next few weeks; I want to make sure I don't encourage her to do too much. On the other hand, I don't want to mollycoddle her if there is no need for it.'

'You've taken to her, haven't you?' said Philip, pleased.

'Yes,' Madeline said.

'And she's taken to you. But as for her going riding or swimming, I don't think you need to stop her. Dr Williams is of the opinion that fresh air and exercise will strengthen her constitution rather than weaken it.'

Madeline nodded. 'Good.'

'But don't feel you have to spend all your time with her. Young girls can be tiresome.'

Madeline remembered that Letitia had said much the same thing, but she did not agree. 'I'm sure Emma could never be tiresome. I want to spend my time with her. How else is she to be made to feel welcome? I want to make sure she enjoys her stay with us. This is her home, after all.'

'Is it, Madeline?' He looked at her intently.

'Of course.' She looked surprised. 'It's only because there has been no mistress here that she has been staying with her aunt. Otherwise she would have been growing up here amongst her family and friends. I am not criticizing,' she hastened to explain. 'I know it wasn't possible for her to stay here whilst you were abroad, but things are different now.'

He leaned back in his shield-backed chair, so that the two front feet of the chair left the floor. 'If it was up to you, would she live here always?'

'She would have to finish her schooling,' said Madeline judiciously. 'I don't think it would be good for her to abandon it, and I'm sure she wouldn't want to. She seems to have many friends. But afterwards, yes, of course. This is her home. It's where she belongs.'

'Even though you would have a young girl — soon turning into a young woman — under your feet all day?'

'I can't see Emma getting under anyone's feet. And as to having a young girl — or a young woman — in the house, why shouldn't I like it?'

'Some women would think of it as competition,' he said, remembering something Letitia had said the year before.

Madeline laughed. 'How could I think of her as competition? Emma is a young girl, whereas I am a married woma . . . ' Her voice trailed away as she realized she was a married woman for another few months only.

'And how are you liking it, being a married woman?' asked Philip penetratingly, ignoring the trailing away of her voice.

Madeline swallowed. The joy had gone out of her conversation. For a few minutes she had been carried away, and had forgotten the true nature of her marriage to Philip, but now she was reminded of it. A few weeks ago the idea that her marriage was temporary had filled her with a feeling of security, but now it created a gaping hole at the heart of her. 'I . . . I like it very well,' she said softly.

'Do you, Madeline?' he asked searchingly.

She nodded mutely.

'Has it been what you expected it to be?' he asked.

'No. But then that is because it is only a temporary marriage,' she replied, remembering her mother's warnings, fainter now, but still there none the less.

'Ah. So that's what you think. You think it would be different if this marriage was permanent?'

'My mother . . . ' she began hesitantly.

'Yes?' he asked.

She did not reply.

'Your mother?' he prompted.

'My mother warned me . . . '

And then the door opened, and Emma walked in.

Philip gave an exclamation of impatience. 'I thought you were going to bed, young lady,' he said.

'I am,' said Emma blithely. 'I just forgot my book.'

She crossed the room to the window-seat, where she had left her latest Gothic novel. Then she tripped over to Philip and kissed him on the forehead.

'Good night, my lord,' she said, mischievously dropping him a curtsy.

'Good night, minx,' said Philip with affectionate exasperation.

'Good night,' she said to Madeline, kissing her on the cheek.

'Good night,' said Madeline, glad to have been interrupted. She was still unsure of herself, still unsure of her own feelings, and still unsure of her mother's warnings. Had those warnings really been necessary? she wondered. Or had they been nothing more than the troubled words of an unhappy woman who had been trapped in an unusually unhappy marriage?

She shook her head. She still did not know for sure.

She stood up, 'I will see you upstairs,' she said to Emma.

'Oh, yes,' said Emma enthusiastically. 'And you can tell me if you have read *The Absentee* yet.'

Talking about Maria Edgeworth's latest novel, the two ladies left the room.

12

Summer ended, and with it Emma's visit. After she had gone, Madeline was surprised at how much she missed her. The two of them had spent many enjoyable days shopping and sightseeing, and had visited every family within ten miles: Emma's lively and affectionate nature had prompted her to see all her friends in Yorkshire before returning to Bath. She had been reluctant to go, but she had her education to complete, and besides, it would not be long before she returned to the manor.

As summer ended, autumn began, and Madeline found that her duties underwent a subtle change. The day-to-day running of the manor was still the same, but she now had also to oversee the bottling of the fruit and the making of jam, together with the other autumnal activities recounted in the old countess's diaries. Perhaps the most important of these was the business of tending to the coughs and colds that were rife on the estate. October was misty and November wet, so that many of the tenants suffered from minor complaints, and some of them from more serious problems such as rheumatism, and she spent much of her time doing what she could to alleviate their suffering. In this she was guided not only by the old countess's diaries but also by Clarissa's practical advice.

Madeline was indebted to Clarissa for a number of home-made remedies, and her first call on a wet and windy morning in November was on Old Ned. The cottage had been repaired since she had first seen it in the summer, and although the repairs were only a temporary measure, designed to make the cottage habitable until a new one could be built, they had made a difference. The cottage was no longer as damp, and the chimney drew better, so that the fire was a respectable blaze. Despite being in pain with rheumatism she found him lively and cheerful, as he always was on her visits.

'Just like 'told days, when her ladyship was still alive,' he said to his wife as he saw Madeline approaching the cottage. To Ned, the phrase 'her ladyship' referred to the old countess, Philip's mother, who had overseen the estate during his time as head gardener.

'How are you feeling this morning?' asked Madeline, putting down her leather saddle-bag on the homely table beside Ned's chair.

'All 'tbetter for seeing you, lass,' he said, leaving Sarah, his wife, spluttering at what she called his 'improperness'.

Madeline, however, laughed. Over the last few months she had grown very fond of Old Ned, and he to revere her with the worship he had previously reserved for the old countess. Mixed with his worship was a sense of fun and a lively appreciation of Madeline's beautiful elfin face.

'Ee, you'll 'ave to forgive 'im,' said Sarah, looking at her husband reprovingly. ' 'e's not 'imself today.'

'I'm not so sure,' said Madeline teasingly. 'He seems every bit himself to me.'

'Aye, lass, tha's in the right of it. If an old man like me can't say what he likes then, I asks you, who can?'

'Did the ointment do any good?' asked Madeline, unpacking the tub of salve she had brought.

'Well, 'tweren't bad,' conceded Old Ned. 'But o' course, 'tweren't as good as a bit of fun.'

'A bit of fun?' asked Madeline, pausing.

'Aye.'

'What kind of fun?' she asked.

'Well, lass,' he said, sending Sarah spluttering again, 'the bit o' fun I was thinking of were in 'tnature of a Christmas fête.'

'Ee, Ned,' said Sarah indignantly. Then, turning to Madeline she said, 'Take no notice, my lady. 'E's been drivelling on

248

about that all week.'

'Proper Christmas parties for the servants and tenants we used to have,' said Ned with a twinkle in his eye. 'When her ladyship was alive.'

Madeline's interest was aroused. She was always eager to learn about the customs of the estate. It had started off as a formality, something she had felt she ought to do in order to make her pose as Philip's wife convincing, but it had quickly become a pleasure, and she had found Old Ned a fountain of knowledge. Being now eighty-two and having lived on the estate all his life he knew more about it than almost anyone else alive, and he liked nothing better than to pass on this knowledge.

With only a little prompting he now regaled Madeline with a full account of the Christmas festivities that used to form an important part of the Stonecrop year before the old Countess had died, but which had since lain dormant.

'And all 'tlads would steer all 'tlasses under 'tmistletoe,' he twinkled at Sarah. 'And that's how I caught me a wife.'

'Ee, Ned, get on with you,' said Sarah, nevertheless very pleased with the memory.

Madeline stayed in the cottage for some time, listening to Ned's tales of Christmas fêtes in years gone by and finding that, the more she thought of it, the more the idea of reviving the custom appealed to her. Ned remembered everything, from the gown the old countess had worn at his first Christmas fête, to the man who had played the fiddle at the last.

So interested did Madeline become that she lost all track of time, remembering at last that she had a dozen more things to see to before dinner and that she must be getting on.

Having made sure that Ned had everything he needed, and having promised that she would visit him again on the following day, she donned her pelisse and gathered up her leather bag before mounting her mare and returning to the manor, accompanied by the faithful Jenkins.

'Old Ned was asking about the Christmas fête,' she told Philip that afternoon as, having been kept inside by the rain, she sat doing a piece of tapestry. 'He wanted to know if the custom was going to be revived.'

Philip looked up from his plans for the home farm. 'The fête,' he said musingly. 'I haven't thought about the Stonecrop fête for years. It's a lot of hard work,' he said meditatively, but there was an unmistakable gleam of enthusiasm in his eyes.

'I should be doing most of that,' said Madeline. 'It's the countess's duty to arrange it, or so Ned told me.'

Philip gave a wry smile. 'Ned's an old rascal. He's right, though. It was my mother, and my grandmother before her, who used to arrange everything, down to the last detail.'

'Well, my lord?' asked Madeline, resting her work on her lap and looking directly at Philip. 'Shall we revive the custom, do you think?'

Philip threw down the plans. 'Why not? Christmas used to be the highlight of the Stonecrop year. It's time we made it so once again.'

'Who comes to the fête?' asked Madeline.

'Everyone. The tenants, the servants, the villagers, they all attend. Jason will be in York again for Christmas,' he said thoughtfully. 'He remembers the fêtes. He will want to come and he will be no doubt willing to help us with the preparations nearer the time. But if we're going to hold the fête we'd better start making the preliminary arrangements at once. I'll have a word with the head groom — the fête is always held in the long barn, and it will need to be cleared for use — if you will have a word with Crump. He will need to know what we are planning.'

The rain had eased off again, and Philip went out to the stables to make sure the head groom remembered what had to be done, whilst Madeline consulted Crump on some of the finer points of the arrangements, Mrs Potts not having been at the manor the last time a fête was arranged. As she did so Madeline reflected on the change the autumn months had made. No longer was she organizing something on her own, or with the aid of servants, as she had done with the ball, now she was arranging it with Philip. They had begun by splitting their concerns down the middle, with Madeline tending to the house and Philip the estate, but now everything had merged into one, and whether it was plans for the home farm, dreams for the gardens, or arrangements for the Christmas festivities, they organized things together.

But not for much longer. Their marriage had almost run its course. The thought of it made her feel bereft. Why was she feeling like this? Why was she not looking forward to moving into the house in York? Why was she not filled with happiness at the thought of having her own home and a generous annuity so that she could live out the rest of her life in comfort and style?

These were the thoughts that plagued Madeline in the weeks leading up to the fête.

★   ★   ★

The date set for the Christmas fête finally arrived.

'Grand, lass,' said Old Ned with a sense of wonder as he looked around the long barn as the party got under way. 'Ee, it's reet grand.'

'Aye, my lady,' said Sarah, his wife. 'Tha's done us proud.'

The barn had been cleared and swept. Chairs had been brought in and set around the sides, so that those who did not wish to dance could sit and watch instead. At the far end, trestle-tables covered in white damask cloths groaned under the weight of hams and cheeses, pies and bread, whilst barrels of ale stood next to them, ready to be consumed. Holly and mistletoe hung in garlands from the rafters, their red and white berries glistening in the candlelight. Everywhere there was noise and chatter. Every servant, every tenant and every villager from miles around was there and the barn was almost bursting at the seams.

Having welcomed everyone with a friendly word Madeline and Philip led the dancing, a fact much appreciated by their guests. There were to be no ballroom dances tonight, no cotillions or minuets, but a fine selection of lively and rumbustious country dances instead.

As the opening chords of *The Shrewsbury*

Lasses filled the air Madeline saw Jason's toes tapping and noticed him looking round for someone. To her delight she realized he was looking for Clarissa. They had both of them enjoyed themselves enormously in the week leading up to the fête, and had come up with a number of joint plans for the decoration of the barn, and now it seemed right they should be dancing together. And how well Clarissa looked tonight, thought Madeline with a warm glance at her friend. But then she had no more time to notice anything else as she gave herself up to enjoyment.

Throughout the evening whilst some danced, others ate, helping themselves to the wholesome fare laid out on the trestle-tables. Meat pies, hunks of bread and whole cheeses were eagerly partaken of, all washed down with flagons of ale.

As the evening drew on, the noise grew. It was many years since a Christmas fête had been held at Stonecrop Manor and it had been sorely missed. Even Jenny, Madeline's maid, was there, and Madeline was pleased to see that she was enjoying herself, dancing with a handsome young groom.

Her eyes wandered round the barn, alighting on Philip. He was chatting to some of the tenant farmers and was at that moment complimenting Mr and Mrs Taylor on their fine son. They had had no one to leave the boy with and had decided to bring him with them, intending to stay for no more than an hour or so before returning home. She saw Philip swing young Tommy Taylor on to his shoulders, whereupon Tommy crowed delightedly to his father, 'I's bigger than you!'

'You'll be having your own children before long,' said Clarissa, who had joined Madeline unawares and was looking adoringly at the little boy. 'It must be the most wonderful feeling to have a little one of your own to play with,' she sighed.

Madeline flushed, a fact Clarissa put down to the countess's modesty, but in fact it was caused by something entirely different. Because Madeline had realized in that moment that she wanted children. And not just any children. Philip's children.

She thought of her mother's warning against marriage, but she had begun to realize that marriage brought with it joys as well as perils.

As she watched Philip playing with Tommy she wanted, with an intensity that surprised her, to give him children. A child of their own to play with; a child to cherish. But it would never happen. Because Philip was self-destined for Letitia.

And suddenly she was angry with him. Why did he want to marry Letitia, a vain and selfish woman who would bring him no joy in life? Why was he being so perverse? Why had he not chosen some loving young woman who would be a companion to him? Who would love and look after his children, instead of banishing them to the nursery as Letitia would do. A young lady who would provide a welcoming home for his sister, and make the manor a warm place that he would want to live in, instead of a cold and glittering showcase. Who would share his hopes and dreams. Who would melt whenever he touched her. Why was he so blind to what would make him truly happy in life? She could not bear it. She wanted the best for him. And the best wasn't Letitia.

But were her feelings really so selfless? she asked herself. Was it just because she wanted the best for Philip that she didn't want him to marry Letitia? Or were her feelings far more personal?

She shivered, and wrapped her arms round herself; it was better not to let her thoughts wander down those channels, but it was becoming more and more difficult to stop them, even though she knew those channels would only lead to heartache. Philip was to marry Letitia; it was all arranged, and she must accept the fact. Because it was not going to change.

With difficulty she turned her attention back to the festivities. She tempted old Mrs Green to a meat-and-potato pie and handed Mr Salter a flagon of ale, but quickly found herself unsettled again when Philip strolled over to her side.

'What is it?' he asked her, drawing her aside, with a perception she wished, at that moment, he did not possess.

'I don't know what you mean,' she said.

'Something's made you angry.'

His face as he looked down into hers was concerned.

'You must be mistaken.'

'No. I've been watching you. Was it something Clarissa said?' he asked.

'Yes . . . I mean no,' said Madeline.

'Yes, you mean no?' asked Philip with a lift of one eyebrow.

'I think we should return to our guests,' said Madeline.

'Not until you've told me what's wrong,' he said.

'It's nothing. It's just that . . . ' The words were unwise, but they had slipped out.

'It's just that . . . ?' he prompted her.

'Nothing.' She made to move past him but he would not let her go.

'If it's nothing, you won't object to telling me,' he said, with a hint of steel in his voice.

She knew she should say nothing; she should laugh it off. But her emotions were still churning and, unwisely, she said abruptly, 'Why are you going to marry Letitia?'

He looked at her appraisingly. Then, seeming to sense some of her feelings, he said, 'We can't talk here.' He led her out of the barn, across the courtyard and in at a side door of the manor house, taking her through into a small room where they could talk undisturbed. 'Now,' he said, closing the door behind them. 'I think you'd better tell me why you care about my reasons for marrying Letitia.'

There was an alert look in his eye and his whole body was tense. He looked like a bird of prey about to swoop, thought Madeline with a shiver. But it was too late for her to keep silent now.

'Why are you not going to marry one of the young ladies from round about?' she asked. 'Why are you going to marry someone so cold and cynical?'

'I wasn't aware it was any of your business,' he remarked.

She had the feeling that for some reason he was deliberately taunting her, though why that should be she did not know.

Before she could reply he went on, 'I will answer your question nevertheless. The reason why I won't marry any of the young ladies from round about is that they would bore me out of my mind. They can talk of nothing but fashions and fripperies. Their ideas are bounded by thoughts of the latest novels, and the latest styles in dress.'

'I thought you liked talking about those things,' she said with a flush, remembering the times she had spoken to him about her new gowns, or about the novel she was reading.

'I do.' With the woman I love, he thought, but did not say it. 'But not to the exclusion of all else.'

'And will Letitia's conversation, then, be so different?' she asked with an attempt at coolness, though her pulse was starting to quicken.

He shrugged. 'Probably not. But she will know better than to bore me with it.'

'And is that all you ask from a wife? That she doesn't bore you?' demanded Madeline.

'That depends.'

'On?' she asked.

'On what sort of wife you are thinking of.'

His eyes drilled into hers, and she dropped them, unable to meet his gaze. 'I . . . I am thinking of a proper wife.'

'Very well.' He turned up her chin so that she was looking at him, and she felt a quiver go through her at his touch. 'From a proper wife I would want friendship and companionship — someone I could share my hopes and dreams with; and a helpmeet — someone who would help me turn those dreams into reality. I would want someone who, besides sharing my interests, had interests of her own, and who would let me help her in her endeavours. I would want someone who was concerned about the tenants and labourers on the estate, and who could talk to them without insulting them or patronizing them And then I would want someone with a strong and courageous character, who would not have a fit of the vapours every time there was a problem in life, but would find a way to solve it. But as well as being strong and courageous she would also have to be soft and vulnerable — I have no taste for harridans! She would have to let me look after her and protect her and make her life easier for her; she would have to rouse in me the desire to make love to her, not just once but over and over again; she would have to be someone I would want to have children with, not just as heirs, but as living, breathing little people of flesh and blood; and she would have to be someone I could imagine spending the rest of my life with and enjoying every minute of it.' His voice dropped. 'Do you know anyone like that, Madeline?'

She gulped. Her pulse was racing and she felt suddenly weak.

'Because if you do, then I won't marry Letitia. I won't need to.' His voice was husky. 'So tell me, Madeline, do you know anyone like that?'

His head was bending towards hers. She could feel the whisper of his breath warm on her cheek. She could smell the fresh, clean scent of him, and beneath it a deeply masculine aroma that made her pulses leap. And then he kissed her.

Madeline was lost in a sea of exhilarating sensations as he pulled her closer to him. It felt right for her to be in his arms. It felt right for him to be kissing her, and for her to be kissing him in response. It felt right for him to be crushing her body to his. And all of a sudden she knew why.

It was because she loved him.

When had it started? she wondered, thinking of the feelings she had for him. Since the moment he had rescued her from her uncle, she realized. And ever since then it had been quietly growing, her friendship and trust and affection for him, her respect and her desire, until those feelings had all merged into one and been transformed into something far more profound; until they had been transformed into love.

And then she could think no more, but gave herself willingly to the delicious sensations that were coursing through her body. As his hands began to caress her she found her sensations intensifying, so that by the time he swept her off her feet and carried her up to the bedroom she was so weak she could not even undress. But his impassioned words and burning kisses told her that he wanted nothing better than to undress her himself.

Philip's lovemaking was the most breathtaking, exhilarating experience, the most wonderful and all-consuming thing she had ever known. And when at last, their passion spent, he cradled her in his arms, Madeline gave a deep sigh of contentment. Nestling into his arms she felt a sense of happiness and fulfilment she had never even dreamed existed.

I have been married to Philip for almost six months, she thought as a pleasurable drowsiness overtook her, but this . . . this has been my wedding night.

13

Philip woke early the following morning. Madeline was asleep beside him. Her long flaxen hair tumbled over the pillow and her face was serene.

He smiled as he remembered how determined he had initially been not to consummate their marriage. But that determination had gone out of the window when he had realized he loved her.

He knew there were still problems to be faced, but whatever the cause of Madeline's fear of marriage he was determined to help her overcome it.

Knowing that Jenny would soon be coming into the room he slipped out of bed and quickly dressed, not wanting to embarrass the little maid. Once dressed he went downstairs and was about to supervise the clearing up after the fête when Crump appeared, saying:

'A messenger has just arrived for you, my lord. He says he has instructions to deliver the message to you and only you. I have put him in the library.'

Philip frowned. A messenger? Who on earth could it be? And who could the message be from? His thoughts went to Jack. If it *was* a message from Jack it could not have come at a worse time, but he could not turn his back on the friend who had saved his life.

'Very good, Crump.'

He strode into the library. A man in ragged clothes stood there. Philip summed him up quickly and decided he was honest. 'Well?' he asked. He wanted to deal with the unwelcome intrusion as quickly as possible so that he could spend the morning with Madeline.

'You're the Earl of Pemberton?' asked the man warily.

'I am.'

'I've got a message for you. 'Meet me same place soon as you can'. That's the message. 'e said you'd know what it meant, and 'oo it was from.'

Philip nodded. So the message *was* from Jack. And if he was sending a coded message he must still be in danger. Philip thought over the wording of the message. Same place — that was easy: the King's Head, the hostelry where they had frequently met and caroused in their youth. And as soon as possible.

It went against all his instincts to leave Madeline at such a time but he knew that Jack would not send him such a message unless it was urgent and he could not let his friend down. Besides, the sooner he went the sooner he would be back. Perhaps even before Madeline woke.

He gave the man a sovereign and then rang for Crump. 'I want a horse waiting for me at the front door in ten minutes,' he said.

'Yes, my lord.'

Once Crump had left the room he went over to the desk and pulled a sheet of paper towards him, taking up his quill and writing a note to Madeline, explaining that he had been called away urgently and saying that he would be back as soon as possible. He signed it, *Your loving husband, Philip*. Then, sanding the note, he went out into the hall. Danson, the footman, was standing there and Philip handed him the note, instructing him to see that it was delivered to the countess as soon as she was awake.

'Yes, my lord,' said Danson deferentially.

But when Philip had gone a cunning look crossed Danson's face. Instead of taking the note to Jenny, so that she could deliver it to her mistress, he went into the servants' quarters and, making sure he was not observed, he stopped in a narrow passageway. Although the passageway was narrow it was well lit: a large window was set into the outside wall. Holding the sealed note up to the light he tried to make out the words of the message. The day was bright, and the light, shining through the paper, revealed much of Philip's bold handwriting. Although it did not reveal every word, Danson could decipher enough of the message to know that Philip had been called away. Thinking quickly, he realized that if Madeline did not receive the note she would not know where the earl had gone. Or why. He cudgelled his brains, trying to think of a way in which that piece of information could be used to create trouble between the earl and the countess, and in so doing help his mistress: not Madeline, but Letitia Bligh. Not for nothing did Miss Bligh pay him a handsome retainer, and not for nothing had she promised him the position of butler once she was firmly established at the manor as its countess.

And then it came to him. An idea so simple and yet so devastating it would end the earl's marriage to Madeline for sure.

Crumpling the note in his pocket with a crooked smile he went into the kitchens, where Jenny was just having her breakfast. It was time for his plan to begin.

'His lordship's out early this morning,' he said to Jenny conversationally.

Jenny, who had seen Madeline and Philip leave the fête together and had drawn her own happy conclusions, did not snub Danson

266

as she usually did, disliking his nosiness, but instead replied cheerfully, 'Perhaps he has work to do.'

'If you can call it that,' said Danson suggestively. 'But I wouldn't call Miss Bligh work. She looks more like pleasure to me.'

'Miss Bligh?' Jenny tried not to rise to his bait, but her heart misgave her.

'That's where he's gone. To see Miss Bligh. I heard him giving orders in the stables. Rumour has it he was about to marry her last year, but instead he came home with another wife. You can't blame him, though, can you? He'd have had to give up the fortune if he'd married Miss Bligh. The old earl was crazy if you ask me. Imagine making a will like that. So what could the earl do? He was in love with Miss Bligh all right, and no wonder, her being so elegant and polished and all — she looks like a countess already, you might say. But marry her and lose the fortune? No. He couldn't bring himself to do it. So he married someone else instead. But feelings will out. Oh, yes, feelings will always out. What is it they say? All's fair in love and war? And I reckon that's about the size of it. He wants Miss Bligh, and one way or another he's going to have her. Oh. But I shouldn't be saying this to you,' he said, appearing to be suddenly contrite. 'I forgot, you came with the mistress, didn't you? I don't suppose it's any joke to you that the master's saddled up and gone to see Miss Bligh.'

'No, you shouldn't be saying this to me,' snapped Jenny. But the damage had been done. Philip and Letitia? Pushing back her stool Jenny threw away the rest of her breakfast.

She found she had lost her appetite.

★ ★ ★

Madeline woke. A smile spread across her face as she remembered the events of the night before. She and Philip . . . it had been so wonderful.

She turned her head, expecting to see Philip beside her, but there was no sign of him. The bed was empty. She felt a moment of intense disappointment, before guessing that he must have already risen and gone downstairs to oversee the servants as they cleared away the debris of the Christmas fête. She could tell it was late by the light streaming through the curtains and she realized she must have overslept.

Even so, she allowed herself a few minutes to indulge in the memory of their blissful night together. How wonderful it had been. She had never known marriage could hold such pleasures. She smiled as she thought how lucky she was. She stroked the pillow next to her. There was a hollow in it where Philip's head had been. The bedclothes still carried the scent of him, warm and masculine. Oh, it was good to be alive!

She threw back the covers and, humming to herself, chose a pale-blue kerseymere gown to wear. It was light and bright, and matched her mood perfectly.

A minute later Jenny came into the room with a jug of hot water.

'Did you enjoy the fête last night?' asked Madeline, as she washed and then set about dressing, with Jenny's help.

'Yes, miss,' said Jenny.

Jenny seemed surprisingly taciturn.

Madeline said teasingly, 'You did not take too much punch, I hope?'

'No, miss.' Jenny seemed not only taciturn but dour.

Madeline frowned. It was not like Jenny to be surly. 'Is anything wrong?' she asked. 'Have you been having trouble with the inquisitive footman again? Danson?'

'No. Nothing's wrong.' Jenny smiled brightly. She did not feel up to telling Madeline what Danson had said. She did not want to trouble Madeline, particularly not now, when she was so happy. And anyway,

Danson could have been mistaken, she told herself, or just making trouble. So ignoring Madeline's comments about the footman she asked, 'Which shawl will you wear this morning? It's a cold day, for all it's bright.'

Madeline looked at the clear blue sky, with here and there a wisp of white cloud, and said, 'Yes. I expect you're right. These bright days are often cold. I think I'll wear the cashmere.'

As Jenny seemed to become her usual self, Madeline said no more and put the maid's initial dourness down to tiredness. Which was not surprising, thought Madeline, as they had all worked very hard to prepare the fête, and had worked even harder to enjoy it.

Once dressed, Madeline went downstairs. She was hoping to see Philip but there was no sign of him and she reasoned he must have breakfasted before her. After finishing her own breakfast she went out to the barn. The servants were clearing up after the fête but none of them seemed to have seen Philip. Still, she was not concerned. He had perhaps been called away to the home farm. One of the prize animals, mayhap, had been taken sick. She missed him and wanted to be with him but knew that he had a lot to do, and it only made her look forward to their next meeting even more. And in the meantime, she had her own activities to occupy her.

Returning to the drawing-room she settled herself down at her escritoire. Taking out a sheet of paper she began to write a letter to Emma, telling the young girl all about the Christmas fête. She had not quite finished when the door opened and Crump appeared.

'Mr Greer is here to see you, my lady,' he said.

'Mr Greer?' Madeline laid down her quill in surprise. What could the manager of the York properties want with her? she wondered. 'I think it must be the earl he wants to see.'

'No, my lady. He asked to see you particularly,' said Crump.

Madeline was puzzled. The only way to find out what Mr Greer wanted, however, was to grant him an interview and so she said, 'Very well, Crump. Show him in.'

A minute later Mr Greer entered the room. Madeline felt a return of her earlier feelings, when she had met Mr Greer for the first time. There was something about the little man she found unsettling. She had not taken to him at all. But telling herself she was being unreasonable she offered him a seat and then said, 'How can I help you, Mr Greer?'

'Oh, no, my lady, it's I who am here to help you,' he said, balancing himself on the edge of a Hepplewhite chair. 'The earl asked me to call on you — '

'You have seen the earl?' asked Madeline in surprise. Philip had not spoken of a recent meeting with his property manager.

'Oh, yes, my lady. I have just left him.'

'You have seen him this morning?' asked Madeline in astonishment.

'Oh yes, my lady, he came over to York first thing. He asked me to give you the keys to the York house. It has been completely redecorated, my lady, and the earl said that now everything is finished you will want to move in straight away.'

Madeline felt an icy feeling stealing over her heart. Surely it could not be true? Philip could not have left her that very morning and ridden over to York, instructing Mr Greer to give her the keys to the York house, could he? After all they had shared? He did not really mean her to move out of the manor? Did he?

But why not? Her marriage to him was a temporary arrangement. She had always known it. He had never made any bones about it. He had not deceived her in any way. But after last night . . .

After last night, what? she demanded of herself. He had taken her to bed, yes, but what did that signify? To her it had signified everything. To him it had signified nothing — she saw that now. He had given into the temptation of the moment and had regretted it. And to put himself beyond the reach of further temptation he had left the manor, arranging for her to move out immediately. Most probably not intending to return until she had gone.

But such cowardice seemed so unlike Philip.

And then her mother's warning, a warning that had almost, but not quite, been stilled over the past few months, came back to haunt her. 'Never trust a man, Madeline. It only leads to despair'.

No, thought Madeline resolutely. She did not accept that. She would not let it lead to despair. She might be devastated; she might feel her heart was breaking; but she could not blame Philip. He had been completely honest with her. He had said all along that he wanted only a temporary marriage leading to an annulment so that he could go on to marry Letitia, and if she had ever imagined, wanted or expected anything else then she had only herself to blame.

She had trusted him, and she had been right to trust him. He had kept to his side of the bargain. He had done everything he had promised. He had provided her with a house and an annuity, and if he wanted her to move into that house now, instead of waiting for the last few days of their six-month marriage to run their course, then why shouldn't he ask it of her? A few days here or there could make no difference. He presumably must think it would make no difference to his inheritance. As long as he presented himself at his lawyer's office on the appointed day, with his wife beside him, he could claim his fortune.

As long as the marriage had not been consummated, that was.

But how were the lawyers to know otherwise? If Philip said the marriage had not been consummated, she was certainly not going to gainsay him. She had too much pride.

But again she felt dissatisfied. It did not seem like Philip at all to act in such a way.

But why else would he send Mr Greer to her with the keys to the York house? she demanded of herself. There was no other explanation.

'Yes. Thank you, Mr Greer.' It was difficult to force the words out, but force them out she did. Her voice, she was pleased to notice, did not wobble or otherwise betray her strong emotion. Instead, it sounded calm and level, as though the idea of her moving into the York house was of no great moment to her.

'Thank you, my lady.'

He handed her the keys and withdrew.

Out in the hall, Mr Greer walked over to Danson, who was lurking there. A bag of gold changed hands. 'You've done well, Danson,' said Mr Greer in an undertone. 'Keeping his lordship's note and sending it to Miss Bligh, instead of giving it to the countess, has been very useful. It's lucky Miss Bligh decided to rent a house nearby when she returned from Scotland, so she could keep an eye on things here. Otherwise you'd never have managed to get a message to her, telling her what you'd done. How did you get it to her, by the way?' he asked curiously.

'By way of one of the stable boys who exercises the horses,' said Danson. 'He was happy to take a note for me and hand it to Miss Bligh's maid.'

'Won't he talk?'

Danson shook his head. 'As far as he knows, all he's done is deliver a message from a lovesick footman to a lady's maid.'

Mr Greer nodded appreciatively. 'A good ruse. Miss Bligh's pleased with you. And when her wedding goes through there'll be another bag of gold for everyone who's helped her. So keep your eyes open and your mouth shut.'

'Look out,' said Danson, as Madeline's footsteps could be heard approaching the other side of the door.

With one last knowing nod Mr Greer slipped out of the house. Danson disappeared into the servants' quarters and Madeline, having taken a few minutes to steady herself and regain her composure, came out of the study knowing nothing of their treachery.

She crossed the hall and mounted the stairs, not giving way to her feelings until she had reached her room. Closing the door behind her, she leant against it, waiting for her strength to return. Then, summoning her courage, she set about doing what must be done. She rang for Jenny and began sorting out her things.

'Ah, Jenny, there you are,' she said, as the maid entered the room.

Jenny looked in surprise at the gowns laid out on the bed.

'I need your help,' said Madeline. 'We are going to the York house a little earlier than expected. I want you to help me pack.'

Jenny, instead of looking surprised, looked tearful. 'So it's true, then.'

'What do you mean?' asked Madeline.

'What Danson said. About *her*.'

'Jenny, what are you talking about?'

'Why are we going to York?' asked Jenny.

'The house is ready. There is nothing to stay here for.' And oh, how much those words cost Madeline. Almost as much as her calm face. 'But what do you mean about it being true?'

'It's just something Danson said,' said Jenny miserably.

'And what did he say?'

'That the earl . . . ' Jenny gulped. 'That the earl had gone to *her*.'

'Her? You mean Miss Bligh?'

Jenny nodded mutely.

'Why didn't you tell me?' asked Madeline, her voice trembling. She had tried to show no feeling but it was too much of a strain.

'I didn't believe him, my lady. I thought he was making mischief. There's something about him I don't like. Are you sure it's true?'

'I don't know where Philip has gone, but it's true he wants us to leave.' She swallowed. 'He sent Mr Greer round with the keys for the house in York.'

'Oh, my lady.'

'Greer of all people,' said Madeline, giving way to her feelings at last. 'I know it is uncharitable of me, but I don't like the man.'

'They're neither of them trustworthy, neither Danson nor Mr Greer, I'm sure of it,' said Jenny. 'Couldn't there be some mistake?'

Madeline shook her head. 'I must confess I hoped so too but there is no mistake. They may not be trustworthy, but Danson has no reason for lying about Philip's whereabouts, and besides, Mr Greer would not dare bring me the keys to the York house unless Philip had asked him to. He knows he would be found out, and then he would lose his position. And even if he dared to do it, why would he want to? What could he hope to gain? Nothing. There could be no reason for him to do such a thing. No, I know of nothing against him, except what my feelings tell me.'

'And mine,' put in Jenny, forgetting her place in her desire to help Madeline.

'Our feelings,' acknowledged Madeline, glad of Jenny's support, 'that tell us he is not trustworthy. But there is no reason for him to lie, as there is no reason for Danson to lie. And besides, if they are lying, then how else can Philip's absence be explained?'

'Maybe he's gone to help his friend,' said Jenny. 'The one who saved his life.' News of the true events surrounding the carriage accident had inevitably leaked out, spreading from the coachmen who had been there at the time to the other outdoor servants and then to the indoor servants, and at last Madeline had revealed the full truth of it to Jenny.

Madeline shook her head. 'If that was the case he would have left me a note. And he would have told Crump where he had gone

— or at least said he'd been called away on urgent business. But when I asked Crump where his master was he told me he did not know. Nor did he know when his master would be back. He only knows that Philip has left the manor. So you see, it must be true. Even if Danson and Mr Greer were playing some deep game they could not make Philip leave the manor. No, Jenny, there is no use looking for reasons to explain away their behaviour. It is all too clear they are telling the truth. Philip feels the marriage is over and has gone to join Miss Bligh. He would like me to leave the manor as soon as possible so that his future can begin.'

I'm sure it isn't like that, Jenny was tempted to say, but did not do so. It would only cause Madeline more pain, and what good would it do?

'Come, let us begin,' said Madeline. 'We should be looking forward to this.' She made an attempt at cheerfulness. 'We will have a beautiful house to live in and we will be together. I will not be married to Lucius Spalding and you will not be turned off as you would have been if my uncle had had his way.'

'Yes, my lady,' said Jenny, stifling a sniff.

'Now, the clothes must be packed carefully . . .'

Three hours later Madeline's things were packed. She partook of a light lunch and then gave orders for the carriage to be brought round. 'I am going to the house in York,' she said to Crump. 'Mr Greer brought the keys for the house round this morning. When the earl returns he will like to know.' She did not say anything further, being sure Philip would like to explain the full details of the situation to Crump himself. Besides, she did not feel equal to it.

'Yes, my lady,' said Crump, with all the poise of a well-trained butler. He showed no surprise, but simply accepted Madeline's orders and saw they were carried out.

Madeline's luggage was loaded up, she took her place in the carriage, and she left the manor.

And as she did so she felt that she left a part of her, the most vibrant, real and important part, behind.

★　★　★

Philip approached the King's Head with caution. Jack's message had necessarily been obscure and he did not know what he might find when he arrived. He did not know what kind of danger Jack found himself in, or what help his friend might need, but he had come prepared. Beneath the folds of his greatcoat he carried two pistols, both loaded and ready for use.

He thought it unlikely that Jack would have gone to the inn itself; the inn was too conspicuous. But there was a derelict cottage just beyond it that would make an ideal meeting place and it was towards this cottage that he turned his horse's head.

He went forward with every sense alert. The cottage appeared to be deserted but he was taking no chances. He dismounted a little way off, looping Nero's reins over a tree before proceeding on foot, moving stealthily towards the back of the building where there were no windows to give warning of his approach. Then, rounding the cottage, he came to the door. With pistols at the ready he kicked it open and went in.

He felt a gun pressed to his temples and a voice said, 'That's far enough.'

Recognizing the voice he said with amusement, 'Is that any way to treat a friend?'

'Philip!' Jack lowered his gun with a grin and shut the door. 'It's good to see you.'

'Not as good as it is to see you, alive and in one piece,' said Philip, clasping Jack's hand. 'When I got your message I feared the worst.'

'You thought you'd find me bleeding to

death?' joked Jack. But despite his devil-may-care attitude there was an underlying tension about him that spoke of a real threat.

'After the incident at Stonecrop, I didn't know what to expect,' said Philip.

Jack nodded. 'It's a pity I couldn't stay and talk to you in person that day, but the pursuit was too hot. Did you get the names to Callaghan?'

'I did.'

'I'm not sure how much Callaghan told you.' Jack looked at Philip questioningly.

'He told me nothing. Callaghan is the proverbial clam.'

Jack grinned. 'In the world of the spy it pays to keep your mouth shut. But if you're to help me you'll need to know everything I've been up to. I've been working under cover for the last six months, trying to discover the identity of a number of double agents who've been passing on information to the French.'

'Ah. So that's it. I suspected it must be something of the kind. They were the names of double agents, then? The names you gave to Madeline?'

Jack's face broke into a sudden grin. 'She's a beauty, Philip. You're a lucky dog.'

Philip's face lit up. 'I know it.' Then he became serious again. 'Tythering and Peters were double agents?'

'Yes. I tried to pass the information on, once I knew for sure, but they found out I was on to them and made it impossible for me to report. They followed me relentlessly. I finally managed to give them the slip and broke into your house in London — '

'So it was you.'

Jack nodded. 'I knew if I could let you know what I'd discovered — that Tythering and Peters were double agents — then you could get the information to Callaghan whilst I led them on a wild-goose chase.' His eyes suddenly gleamed. 'You really should have better catches on your windows!' he laughed. 'It was child's play to break in!'

'But something went wrong?' said Philip.

'Unfortunately, yes. They caught up with me just as I put a leg over the window sill. It gave me a shock, I can tell you, when I saw their dark shapes skulking through your garden. It's a good thing the moon was up, or I might have missed them.'

'And so you left in a hurry?'

'I jerked my leg back out of the window post-haste,' agreed Jack. He grinned. 'If I remember correctly, I owe you a vase.'

'It was an ugly thing. I'm glad to be rid of it,' said Philip wryly, remembering the vase that had been smashed on the night of the break-in. If Jack had had to leave in a hurry it was no wonder something had been knocked over. Then he turned his attention back to the present. 'Tythering and Peters followed you away from the house?'

'They did. I gave them the slip a dozen times, but they always caught up with me again.'

'As Peters caught up with you at Stonecrop?'

'Yes. But by good fortune I was able to get their names to Madeline. It's lucky you were able to get the message to Callaghan.'

'I went one better than that. I got Peters to him as well.'

Jack wanted to hear all about it, and briefly Philip told him how Peters had been caught.

'Then my work is almost done,' said Jack. 'I've trailed the other suspects and found one further double agent.' He drew a crumpled piece of paper out of his coat pocket and handed it to Philip. 'See that this gets to Callaghan as well, will you?'

'Why not take it to him yourself? Or is Tythering still on your tail?'

'Not Tythering. Something worse. He tired of the chase and hired a band of cut-throats to track me down.'

Philip's eyes narrowed. 'I wonder . . .'

Jack looked at him questioningly.

'When Madeline and I were travelling to Yorkshire we were stopped by a group of six armed ruffians. They wore scarves over their faces, but they weren't common highwaymen. I wonder if they were the same men.'

'If not the same, then at least men like them.'

'Why did they hold us up?' asked Philip. 'Do you know?'

'Not for certain. But I should imagine they thought your journey to Yorkshire was a cover for smuggling me out of the capital.'

Philip nodded. 'That makes sense. They searched the coach, presumably thinking you were inside. And then slashed the squabs in order to make sure the seats were not false, and hiding you. But how does the situation stand with you now?' he asked.

'I've shaken them off for the moment, and I'll be returning to London as soon as I get the chance. But I need you to be my insurance. I want to be certain the final name gets to Callaghan, even if I don't make it.'

'You can count on me for that. If you need help with the men following you . . . '

Jack laughed and clapped him on the back. 'I can look after myself.'

'A pity,' said Philip. 'I was hoping I might get a chance to repay my debt.'

'You're out of luck. No life saving needed

today. Maybe . . . ' Jack broke off, his body suddenly tense. Outside, a twig had cracked.

Philip had heard it, too, and was instantly alert. Raising one of his pistols he went over to the window. Jack approached it from the other side. The two men looked out.

Nothing.

No horses. No people. No sign of movement.

But they had both heard the twig cracking.

Someone was out there.

And then everything happened at once. The door was kicked open, a shot was fired and Jack, having discharged his pistol and killed his opponent in return, gave a cry and slumped to the ground. At the same moment Philip fired through the window where a second man had appeared, pistol raised and ready to fire. The man gasped and then collapsed.

With the two cut-throats neutralized, Philip lost no time in going over to his prostrate friend. 'How bad is it?' he asked, bending over Jack to examine the hole in his side.

'Not . . . not . . . bad,' said Jack from between gritted teeth. 'Don't . . . think it . . . got anything . . . vital.'

But for all his brave words, both men knew if Jack did not get help, and get it soon, he would bleed to death.

'Here.' Philip tore off his cravat and formed it into a pad, holding it against Jack's wound. 'Press down hard. Once the bleeding's stopped I'm taking you to the inn.'

Jack's hand clutched at Philip's arm. 'No. There . . . there were . . .'

There was a slight sound behind him. Philip whirled on instinct and discharged his second pistol. Not a moment too soon. Another cut-throat had entered the cottage. The man's eyes widened as Philip's bullet found its mark. His gun fell to the floor. Then his knees buckled and he toppled over, falling across his dead comrade.

' . . . three . . . of them,' Jack finished with a weak smile.

'Don't talk,' said Philip. 'Save your strength.'

Jack only shook his head. 'Looks like . . . good day . . . for repaying debt . . . after all,' he said.

★ ★ ★

A good day for repaying my debt, thought Philip some hours later, as he left the King's Head. Yes, it was.

Having taken Jack to the inn and seen him attended to by the best doctor in the area, and having given the innkeeper a bag of gold to look after him — with the promise of a second bag as long as Jack made a good recovery — Philip set out for Hull.

As he rode out of the inn yard he was glad he did not have to ride all the way to London. It was fortunate that Callaghan had given him his itinerary when he had travelled to London earlier in the year, and even more fortunate that Callaghan was at present in the north. Which meant that Philip should be able to give him the information about the final double agent, and give him news of Jack, whilst still arriving back at Stonecrop in time for Christmas.

*   *   *

Two days later Philip reined in his horse, his mission to Callaghan completed. He sat still, drinking in the view of the manor from his vantage point high on the Yorkshire moors. Somewhere inside it was Madeline, longing for him as he was longing for her. He had been away longer than he'd expected when he'd set out — two days in all — but it was still only 24 December. As he'd hoped, he was home in time for Christmas.

He set off again, towards the manor.

'Welcome back, my lord,' said Crump as Philip strode through the door.

'Thank you, Crump,' said Philip, pleased to be home ahead of the snow that threatened to fall from the heavy sky overhead. 'Where is the countess?' he asked, as he divested himself of his many-caped greatcoat and his riding-gloves.

'She has gone to York, my lord.'

'Good,' said Philip, thinking she must have gone shopping and pleased that she was enjoying a little relaxation after all her hard work organizing the fête. 'Did she say when she'll be back?'

'I believe, my lord, that she does not intend to come back. Mr Greer was here,' explained Crump, seeing Philip's shocked expression, 'and I believe he handed over the keys to the house in York. Her ladyship left a few hours later, my lord.'

'When was this?' demanded Philip. This was far from the happy homecoming he had expected.

'Two days ago, my lord. Shortly after you had left.'

'Thank you, Crump,' said Philip. He was unwilling to display any emotion in front of his trusted butler and retired to the library where he knew he would not be disturbed.

Why had she gone to York? he asked himself. Had she objected to him helping Jack? No. He didn't believe it. Had he frightened her by taking her to bed? No. He remembered her response too clearly for that. She had not been frightened but had rejoiced in their union, as he had.

But why, then, had she sent for the keys to the York house? And why had she left the manor without any explanation?

He refused to give way to the sense of loss that threatened to engulf him. There must be a reason for her leaving. Was she still afraid of marriage? Was that why she had left? he wondered. Had she guessed he meant to ask her to make the marriage real? And had she been frightened by the idea? He did not know. But he was determined to find out, because he was too deeply in love with Madeline to draw back now. He must go to York; find her; speak to her. Whatever her fears, he would help her to overcome them.

Without stopping to rest he called for a fresh horse and as the sky darkened overhead he set out for York.

★ ★ ★

To begin with, Madeline had hoped that Philip might follow her to York, but as the days passed the unrealistic dream faded. Finally realizing that she must try and let go of the past she turned her energies into making the York house as homelike as she could, whilst Jenny set about buying provisions, and then she devoted her thoughts to the festive season. She had hoped to be spending Christmas at the manor but as it was not to be, she must make the York house as festive as possible. It would cheer both her and Jenny if the house was decorated. With this end in mind she decided to go out and gather some greenery. She intended to come home with a large basketful to surprise Jenny. It would lift their spirits to tuck holly behind the mirrors and trail ivy round the candlesticks.

Telling Jenny that she was going out to run some last-minute errands she selected a large basket from the kitchen whilst Jenny fetched her outdoor things. She was just about to don her pelisse when there was a knock at the door and Jenny went to answer it. A minute later the little maid returned.

'Miss Bligh, my lady,' she said woodenly.

'My dear Madeline,' said Letitia, walking into the room a second later looking every bit as elegant as usual. Her cloak was made of the finest wool and was lavishly trimmed with fur. Beneath it she wore a fashionable pelisse and underneath it a glimpse of her silk walking-dress could be seen. On her head was perched an exquisite feathered bonnet.

Madeline felt herself grow hot and then cold. What was Letitia doing here? 'Miss Bligh,' she said with a calmness she was far from feeling.

Letitia looked round the room. 'This really is a beautiful house,' she said. 'And how well you have settled in.'

Letitia's tone was patronizing, and Madeline wondered once again how Philip could be so determined to marry her. Letitia would not make him happy. Madeline caught herself up for thinking about things that were not her concern.

'But you were about to go out,' said Letitia, seeing Madeline's pelisse and cloak.

'Yes.' Madeline gave an inward sigh of relief that her cloak and pelisse were in the room. A prolonged visit from Letitia would have tried her self-control to the utmost. 'I was about to go and collect some greenery to decorate the house.'

'What an excellent idea. I know a good spot on the other side of the river. There is a holly bush, and plenty of ivy. There used to be mistletoe as well. In fact, I think I will go with you. I need a little more myself. Besides, it is on the way to my carriage.'

It was the last thing Madeline wanted, but she could not prevent Letitia from accompanying her. She put on her outdoor clothes, pulled on her gloves and caught up her basket, then the two women went out into the winter's day. A soft covering of snow lay on the ground. It was beautiful. If she had been alone Madeline would have been enjoying the scene. As it was, she felt on edge.

'I expect you're wondering why I have come,' said Letitia, breaking off a moment later to guide Madeline towards a tributary of the river. 'But I just had to thank you for all you've done for us. Without you Philip would not have been able to claim his fortune and we would not have been able to marry.'

Madeline said nothing. Letitia clearly wanted to torment her but she was not prepared to let her unhappiness show.

The sky darkened, and more snow began to fall. Soft large flakes drifted lazily down from the sky.

'We go across the bridge,' said Letitia, pointing out the narrow wooden span. It was not designed for horse-traffic, and was wide enough for only one person to walk across at a time. It was covered with a thick layer of snow, and more flakes were falling all the time. Letitia looked up at the dark sky. 'Perhaps we had better quicken our pace.'

They had almost reached the bridge when Letitia gave an impatient exclamation. 'My bootlace has come undone. No, don't wait.

The weather is growing worse. I will catch you up.'

Madeline went on ahead, hurrying through the worsening snow to the bridge. She began to cross, meaning to wait for Letitia on the other side. But she had hardly gone half-way when there was an ominous splintering sound and the wood beneath her gave way. She tried to jump to the sound wood beyond but the bridge was slippery and she missed her footing, dropping through the gaping hole that had opened in the middle of the bridge. The basket fell out of her hand and plunged into the icy water racing below, but she managed to catch hold of one of the bridge-supports with her right hand. For a moment she hardly dared breathe as she hung suspended above the fast-moving waters, but the support was sound and bore her weight. The first shock of the fall past, she swung herself a little, trying to build up enough momentum to carry her other hand close enough to the bridge to gain another handhold.

She tried and failed, but to her relief she saw that Letitia had tied her lace and had reached the bridge. Even now, Letitia was making her way carefully across, testing her footholds cautiously before committing her full weight to a new plank, until she stood almost directly above Madeline.

'Hold on to the handrail,' called Madeline, 'and then give me your other hand.' For the first time in her life she was grateful for Letitia's presence.

But instead of making any move to help her, Letitia looked down at her with cold, hard eyes. 'Give you my hand? Why would I want to do that?'

Madeline's face registered her shock, and Letitia gave a cold, mirthless laugh.

'How sad!' she said. 'The noble countess swept away by the current on Christmas Eve! It quite breaks my heart.'

'Help me up,' cried Madeline, thinking that the shock had turned Letitia's mind.

'Help you up? So that you can steal from me everything that is rightfully mine? Oh, no, Madeline. I am not going to sink into poverty and obscurity whilst you run the manor. Stonecrop is mine. I am going to be the Countess of Pemberton and neither you nor anyone else is going to stand in my way.'

'But you already have it,' said Madeline, her arm aching with the strain of hanging beneath the bridge, wondering what Letitia could possibly mean. 'In a few more days Philip will be able to claim his fortune and then he will have the marriage annulled and you will have everything you want.'

'Everything I want?' Letitia's voice was amazed. But then she began to laugh. 'How rich! You don't know, do you! Oh! It's too rich, it really is! You still think Philip means to marry me.' Her laughter degenerated into giggles. 'It is too fine a jest! Philip has no intention of marrying me. He is in love with you. He has been in love with you for months. And you haven't even realized it!'

'In love with me?' asked Madeline in astonishment. But then her astonishment faded as she realized that what Letitia was saying was true. 'Philip is in love with me,' she said. A smile washed over her face. She was hanging from a broken bridge with the icy waters of the river running beneath her and her tormentor above her, and yet life in all its strangeness was giving her the happiest moment she had ever known. Philip was in love with her. For one wonderful moment that thought blotted out everything else.

'Yes.' Letitia's ground-out word brought her back to the reality of her situation. 'In love with you.'

'Then . . . he didn't go to you?'

Letitia's smile was malicious. 'That was a good touch, was it not? It was Danson who thought of it. He kept the note that Philip wrote for you, explaining where he had gone and why. After that, it was a simple matter to make you think he had gone to me. A few choice words to your maid, and the damage was done.'

'But Mr Greer . . . ?' asked Madeline.

'Ah yes. Mr Greer. Mr Greer has been very useful one way and another. It was an easy matter to persuade him to take you the keys of the York house so that you would think Philip wanted you to move out of the manor — Mr Greer will do anything for money.'

'But why?' gasped Madeline.

'Isn't it obvious? I knew you would be much more vulnerable here than you would be at Stonecrop, where you had a house full of servants, to say nothing of the faithful Jenkins, watching over you.'

Jenkins! If only she had not told him she would no longer be needing his services now that she was moving to York, thought Madeline miserably.

'Besides, I knew this bridge was rotten,' went on Letitia. 'It was the perfect way to dispose of you.'

'But when Philip returns . . . ' protested Madeline.

'He will find you are dead. Leaving the way open for him to marry me.'

'No!' Madeline thought desperately for a way to dissuade Letitia. 'The marriage hasn't run its course. Philip won't be able to claim his inheritance if you let me drown.'

'I'm sure the lawyers won't quibble over a day or two in the face of your sad demise. But if they do, well, Philip will still be able to make me a countess, if not a fabulously wealthy one. Now, if you'll excuse me, I can't stand here all day. Goodbye, Madeline.'

'No!' called Madeline.

But Letitia was already making her way back across the bridge, and was soon swallowed up by the whirling snow.

Alone again, Madeline realized that no one would be coming to help her. Steeling herself for the effort she tried to pull herself up on to the bridge. Once, twice, three times she tried, but her arms were not strong enough, and on the fourth attempt she slipped and fell into the icy waters below.

But even as the river closed over her head she did not give up. Philip loved her. And she was determined to fight with every last ounce of her strength for life.

★ ★ ★

A feeling of foreboding overcame Philip as he strode towards the river. He had ridden to the York house on leaving the manor but once there he had found that Madeline had just gone out. And worse, he had discovered that she had just gone out with Letitia. His conversation with Jenny had filled him with unease. Why had Letitia visited Madeline? To make mischief? His mouth set in a grim line.

His strides became longer as he followed the path Letitia and Madeline had taken. Thank God he could not be too far behind them. He had learnt from Jenny that Letitia had told Madeline there was a good spot for greenery on the other side of the river, and by dint of questioning the few people who were out on the streets in the snow, finishing their last minute purchases for the festive season, he was able to discover exactly which way they had gone and then to follow. He was drawing near a tributary of the river now, and could see the bridge that spanned it. And on it — could that be Letitia? Yes. Despite the swirling snow he recognized her by her height. But she was hurrying back across the bridge and was swallowed up by a sudden flurry. Philip did not give her a second thought. It was not Letitia he wanted to find, it was Madeline. But where was she? He quickened his step, just as he heard a loud splash and looking into the fast-flowing waters saw Madeline surface for a split second before being carried away.

And then he was flinging off his greatcoat and dragging off his boots and plunging into the water after her. Conditioned as he was he still felt the icy water numbing him and struck out with strong, powerful strokes, knowing that even if she did not drown Madeline could not long survive the cold. He saw her up ahead of him making a valiant effort to catch at the protruding branch of a tree, but it was rotten and snapped in her hand. But it had slowed her enough for Philip, with one strong kick of his legs, to reach her. He caught her arm, pulling her towards him as he trod water until he could get a more secure hold, then, fighting the rushing river, he swam with her to the bank and lifted her out.

She had just enough strength left to haul herself further up the bank, away from all danger of being dragged into the water again, before she collapsed.

She had swallowed a lot of water and was numb with cold but she was alive.

Following her out of the water Philip wrapped her in his coat and then, sweeping her up into his arms, he strode back to the house.

As Jenny opened the door and saw Madeline lying so still in Philip's embrace she let out a gasp of horror, but then responded quickly to Philip's commands.

'Bring me blankets,' he said as he took her

into the parlour, 'and then fetch Dr Morris.' Quickly he gave Jenny directions for finding the doctor and Jenny, barely stopping to put on her cloak, ran out into the snow.

'Madeline,' said Philip, chafing her hands and feet. 'Madeline. Come back to me.'

At last the doctor arrived and examined her whilst Philip paced up and down the room.

'Well?' he demanded as the doctor rose, looking grave.

'It's difficult to say. Her pulse is steady and with care she should recover but there may be problems to come. Pneumonia, fever — but then we will face that if, and when, it happens.'

'Bring her back to me, Doctor,' said Philip, his face etched with worry.

'I'll do all I can. Now this is what I want you to do.' He spoke to both Philip and Jenny, giving them instructions for Madeline's care, saying to Philip, 'And you must get out of those wet things yourself, at once. You may have a strong constitution, but you won't escape unscathed if you delay.'

Philip nodded.

'You'll be needing some help from the manor, I don't doubt. I'll send my lad. You should have someone here before night falls.'

'Thank you. This house isn't equipped for emergencies.'

'I'll see myself out,' said the doctor.

And then Philip carried Madeline up to her room and left Jenny to undress her whilst he stripped off his wet things, returning wrapped in a blanket to keep a watch over his beloved wife.

14

Madeline woke to find Philip sitting in a chair beside her bed. As she saw the rhythmic rise and fall of his muscular chest she realized that he was asleep. And no wonder, she thought; he looked tired. There were dark circles beneath his eyes and he was unshaven, something she had never known before. But his presence was comforting, and as weakness overtook her she slipped back into sleep, made easy now by the knowledge that he was by her side.

She woke again sometime later, feeling stronger. She was able to make sense of her surroundings and realized that she was in her bedroom in York.

The events of the last — day? week? — came flooding back to her: Letitia's visit, their walk through the snow, and the splintering of the rotten footbridge. She shivered as she remembered how she had hung helplessly from its support, and her panic as she had finally lost her grip. And then her memory dissolved into a confused jumble of images: the icy water and her desperate struggle to keep afloat, then her relief as someone had caught hold of her, and her joy as she had realized that that someone was Philip.

'Well, well,' said Philip, seeing she was awake. Leaving the chair in which, had she but known it, he had kept a constant vigil for the past five nights he went to sit beside her on the bed. He took her hand and then, bending over her, he kissed her on the cheek. 'It seems I can't let you out of my sight for a minute! You gave me quite a fright.'

Madeline sensed that his words were deliberately light. She may have regained consciousness but she could tell she was far from well. She had only a hazy memory of what had happened, but she remembered enough to know that she had been ill following her plunge into the icy river. Seeing how drawn his face was, and realizing how worried he had been about her, she wondered whether it was possible, as Letitia had claimed, that he was in love with her? Or had she just imagined it? Had her fevered mind invented that part of the conversation? Until she had heard the words from his own lips she could not be sure.

'I feel a little strange,' she said, trying to echo his lightness.

'You will do. You've been running a fever, but it's broken now. All you need is plenty of rest. And I mean to make sure you get it,' he said, tucking her hand back under the covers.

His touch was strong and comforting. Madeline smiled at him and then drifted back into sleep.

★   ★   ★

Madeline's convalescence was slow. To begin with she was content to lie in bed, drifting in and out of sleep, but by and by she became stronger, and at last was ready to go downstairs.

Philip carried her down himself, setting her gently on the elegant *chaise-longue* in the sitting room. She was able to read and, later, to enjoy receiving visitors, as many as the doctor — and Philip — would allow. He stood watch over her, and if he saw that she was tiring he brought the visits to an end.

Sarah, Old Ned's wife, was Madeline's first visitor. She refused to sit down, despite Madeline's entreaties, and said she'd just called to deliver a jar of calves-foot jelly.

'Turnabout's fair play,' she chuckled, remembering the time in the autumn when Madeline had taken her a jar of the same jelly to help her get over a nasty cold.

Madeline thanked her, and, as she did so,

she caught sight of Philip's pleased expression. He had always been glad that she had got on so well with the tenants and labourers on the estate, and Madeline herself was pleased, too. She was very fond of the 'Yorkshire folk' as Jenny called them, and she was interested to hear all about Sarah's Christmas, and to learn that Old Ned's rheumatism was responding well to the new ointment he was trying.

Clarissa and Jason were the next to call. Over the ensuing days, as Madeline gradually regained her strength and vigour, they were frequent visitors to the house in York. They kept her entertained with stories of their Christmas and New Year, never over-tiring her but lifting her spirits and making her feel how fortunate she was to have such good friends.

Towards the end of January, when Madeline had almost fully recovered, Clarissa and Jason paid another visit, and this time there was an air of suppressed excitement about them.

'You'll never guess,' said Clarissa, beaming at Madeline.

Madeline looked from Clarissa to Jason, and back again. They had become almost inseparable over the last few weeks, and, seeing Clarissa's beaming face, Madeline guessed what she was about to say. 'You mean . . . ?' she began.

'Yes,' burst out Clarissa, proudly displaying a ring, 'Jason and I are to be married!'

Madeline had begun to suspect an attachment on seeing the two of them together during their visits to her and was overjoyed that her suspicions were correct. A few months ago, the idea that Clarissa was about to be married would have horrified her, but now she was delighted to know that Clarissa was going to become Jason's wife. She congratulated her friend with a real and genuine warmth. It seemed strange to her now that she had been so afraid of marriage. She had come to realize that it held joys as well as terrors, and to realize that happy marriages existed, so that she was able to give Clarissa and Jason her heartiest congratulations.

'And just when I had resigned myself to being on the shelf!' said Clarissa.

'Love is no respecter of age,' remarked Philip, his eyes fixed warmly on Madeline, for no matter how young she was he had fallen in love with her.

Clarissa looked from Philip to Madeline and back again, and with a pleased smile playing around her lips she took her leave. 'For I have a hundred and one things to do;

we mean to be married as soon as possible,' she said as she parted from them.

'And what about *our* marriage?' asked Philip, when Clarissa had left.

'*Our* marriage?' asked Madeline, feeling her pulse begin to quicken.

'I have not spoken of it to you before now,' said Philip, sitting down beside her and taking her hand in his. 'You were ill, the doctor had ordered you complete rest, and I did not want to unsettle you in any way.' He hesitated for a moment, then said, 'Madeline. I don't want our marriage to end.'

Madeline caught her breath. She thought of what Letitia had said on the bridge, that Philip loved her, and wondered if it could be true. But Philip himself had not said anything to her of love.

Misunderstanding the catch in her breath, and thinking she was afraid at his mention of a permanent marriage, he asked, 'Why is it you fear marriage?' Adding, 'You do fear it, don't you?'

She nodded.

'Won't you tell me why you are afraid?'

'My parents' marriage was not a happy one,' she said slowly. 'My father treated my mother very badly. He belittled her at every opportunity, particularly in front of other people. It was as though he wanted to show everyone how much power he had over her. And of course he had. He was her husband, she his wife. He made her life a torment. He contradicted her at every turn. He pretended to want to know her opinion and then if she dared express it he treated it with contempt. He bullied her unmercifully. He never let her go out and did not allow her to have any friends. And she warned me — over and over again she warned me — never to marry. Marriage, she said was a trap.' She shuddered. 'What I saw and heard in my childhood, together with my mother's warning, made me determined never to marry. Once a husband has control of a wife he descends into cruelty and she is lost. Or so my mother said.'

'Is that what you think would happen if our marriage became real?' he asked.

She frowned. 'I cannot believe it.'

'But still you fear it,' he said, sensing it was so and wanting to help Madeline overcome the last of her fears. And he knew exactly how to do it. 'Has our marriage descended into cruelty over the last few weeks?' he asked.

She looked puzzled. 'No. But then ours is a sham of a marriage.'

'No. Not any more. For the last three weeks it has been real. You have lost track of time, Madeline. It is almost the end of

January; it is 1813 no longer, but 1814. I claimed my inheritance weeks ago. Because of your illness the lawyers came over to the house on the appointed day, instead of expecting us to go to their offices, and, bearing witness to the fact that I was married, and had been so for six months, they made the Rochdale fortune over to me. So you see, Madeline, for the last three weeks our marriage has been real.'

'Real,' she breathed.

'Yes. Real.' He took her hand. 'Has it turned into a nightmare because it is real?' he asked her, looking deep into her eyes.

She shook her head as she felt a warm glow stealing over her. 'No, it hasn't.'

'And it never will. Because I love you, Madeline,' he said.

'As I love you,' she returned, feeling a great surge of happiness. But then an unwelcome thought occurred to her. 'Letitia . . . '

'I was never in love with Letitia — ours was to have been a marriage of convenience, a suitable match — but when I realized I loved you I told her I could never marry her. I would have told you at the time, but I did not want to cause you anxiety. I knew you felt safe with me because you thought our marriage was temporary, and I did not want to take that feeling of safety away from you.'

'So that is why she tried to kill me,' said Madeline.

'Yes. I should have guessed she would do something like this. I thought at the time she seemed to take the news too calmly. I had expected her to rant and rave. But instead she said, quietly, that she knew I loved you, and that she was not surprised I wanted to bring our — hers and my — agreement to an end. I was amazed at her coolness and even commented on it but she said there would be no use her making a fuss as it would not change anything and so she would wish me well instead. I should have suspected she had something planned, but I honestly believed that she had accepted the situation.'

'You couldn't have known,' Madeline said.

'No, you're right, I couldn't have known. If I had thought about it I could have guessed that she might make mischief, but I could never have guessed she would try and kill you. I knew she wanted to be a countess, but I never suspected that her ambition would carry her so far.'

'She thought that, if I was out of the way, you would return to her,' Madeline explained.

Philip shook his head. 'I would never have done so. I had realized my mistake in thinking I could ever marry her. It's strange, I think my father knew I would. I think that's why he put the awkward clause in the will, stipulating that I would not inherit the Rochdale fortune if I married her. He wanted me to have the happiness he had had in life, you see, and to experience a love-based marriage, and he knew that with Letitia I could never do that. And so he made it almost impossible for me to marry her. He knew I would never give up the fortune willingly in order to marry her, because I needed it to improve the estate, and so he reasoned that I would find a way round the awkward clause. And I think he knew that this would be the way I would find: that I would take a convenient young lady as a temporary wife. But knowing me as he did, I think he knew that I would never go through with a sham of a marriage unless somewhere, deep at the heart of me, I knew it to be real.'

Madeline nodded. 'I knew it, too. I didn't realize it at the time but I could never have made those vows if I had not, somewhere deep inside of me, known you were the man I wanted to spend my life with,' she said, nestling into his arms.

He kissed her softly on the top of her head.

'Do you know?' he said, 'I think I've loved you from the moment I first saw you at Lady Appleton's ball. That night, although I didn't know it then, was the start of my life. I was so proud of you when we came to the manor.

You seemed to belong there, as though you were a part of the estate. And you seemed to belong in my arms. Despite the fact I wasn't meant to be touching you, I couldn't help it,' he smiled. 'You were just so beautiful. And then when Stuart had the audacity to suggest you should become his wife . . . '

Madeline looked at him in surprise.

'Aunt Honoria told him that our marriage was a sham,' he said. 'And suggested he marry you when your marriage to me was done.'

Madeline was amazed. 'So that is why he paid so much attention to me. I never knew.'

'She did it on purpose, of course, to make me acknowledge what I felt for you. And it worked.'

'So that is why Stuart never visited us again!' laughed Madeline.

'I'm afraid I sent him off with a flea in his ear.'

He held her close.

'But I didn't want to tell you of my feelings until the six months had run their course,' he went on. 'I knew you were happy and I did not want to do anything to spoil that. I thought if I could show you how warm and fulfilling marriage could be then I could overcome your aversion to being my wife.'

'To being a wife,' she corrected him. 'Not

to being your wife.'

'And then I had to go away.'

Madeline turned to him curiously. 'Why *did* you go away. You have never explained.'

Briefly, Philip told her about Jack's message. 'And so I wrote you a note explaining my absence — '

'Which was never delivered, because the footman, Danson, was in Letitia's pay,' said Madeline. 'I should have given more credence to my suspicions. Jenny had warned me about his inquisitiveness, and I myself had found him kneeling outside a door. But at the time I believed what he had wanted me to believe, that he had been searching for a button, instead of realizing that he had been spying on us and trying to gauge how far our relationship had gone.'

'Yes. Danson was in Letitia's pay. As was Mr Greer. But you need not be afraid of seeing them again: they have both of them been dismissed. At the time, however, I didn't know that Danson was in Letitia's pay and I assumed you would get the note, and that you would understand why I had had to leave. And so I went to help Jack.'

He told her of everything that had happened at the cottage behind the King's Head.

'Was Jack badly hurt?' asked Madeline. She

was concerned for the man who had saved Philip's life.

'He was, but I sent for the doctor and stayed with him until he was out of danger.'

'Then it really is over,' said Madeline.

'Yes. It is. Jack has completed his mission. There will be no more mysterious break-ins or masked men holding us up on the highway, no more shots in the grounds or vicious horsemen; my debt to Jack is paid.'

'And what of Letitia? Will she return to plague us?'

'No. She has accepted the hand of the old Duke of Garton. She wanted a title and a fortune, and by her marriage she will have both. She will become a Duchess, and as the Duke is over seventy years old I have no doubt she is hoping she will soon be a wealthy widow.'

Madeline sighed. It would be useless to try and bring Letitia to book for what she had done, as there was no proof; but at least, married to the Duke of Garton, Letitia would never try something so heinous again. She would have a reputation and a position in society to protect. 'The Duke should suit Letitia,' said Madeline.

'On the face of it, yes, but not underneath.' Philip laughed. 'The Duke is notoriously tight-fisted, and never spends a penny of his money if he can help it! And although he is over seventy, if he takes after his father he will live until he is almost a hundred years old! But still, that is not our problem. The Duke lives in Edinburgh, and Letitia will live there with him. Our paths will not cross again.'

Madeline rested her head on Philip's shoulder. 'It's strange. Letitia sought to hurt me, but in the end she did quite the opposite. She told me that you loved me, thinking to mock me as I was about to die. But instead of crushing my spirit with the news she only strengthened it. If not for that, I might not have had the courage to struggle as hard as I did, but once she had told me I knew I must do everything I could in order to save myself. Because at that time I didn't know — ' She stopped abruptly and sat up.

'Didn't know?' he asked her.

'At that time, I didn't know that I was with child.'

A broad smile crossed his face. 'And the baby?' he asked.

'Is safe,' she said. 'I didn't want to tell you before I was sure, in case anything happened, but now that I am well on the road to recovery the doctor says there is nothing to fear.'

Philip placed his hand gently on her stomach. 'A child,' he said.

Madeline put her hand over his, and felt a warm feeling of love and happiness flood her whole being. So this is marriage, she thought. A real marriage. Not one based on cruelty and power. Not one based on the need for an inheritance. But one based on love.

If only my mother's marriage had had the same base, thought Madeline, she need never have suffered as she did. It was not marriage that undid my mother, but a marriage without love.

And as she realized that she finally laid all the ghosts of her mother's warnings to rest.

'I offered you my hand once before, for six months,' said Philip. 'Now I offer it to you for life. Will you accept it, Madeline?'

'Oh, yes, Philip,' she said. 'I will.'

Their six-month marriage was over. And as Madeline nestled into Philip's arms she looked forward to all the joys and challenges their lifelong marriage would bring.

We do hope that you have enjoyed reading this large print book.

Did you know that all of our titles are available for purchase?

We publish a wide range of high quality large print books including:
Romances, Mysteries, Classics
General Fiction
Non Fiction and Westerns

Special interest titles available in large print are:
The Little Oxford Dictionary
Music Book
Song Book
Hymn Book
Service Book

Also available from us courtesy of Oxford University Press:
Young Readers' Dictionary
(large print edition)
Young Readers' Thesaurus
(large print edition)

For further information or a free brochure, please contact us at:
Ulverscroft Large Print Books Ltd.,
The Green, Bradgate Road, Anstey,
Leicester, LE7 7FU, England.
Tel: (00 44) **0116 236 4325**
Fax: (00 44) **0116 234 0205**

Other titles in the
Ulverscroft Large Print Series:

THE UNSETTLED ACCOUNT

Eugenia Huntingdon

As the wife of a Polish officer, Eugenia Huntingdon's life was filled with the luxuries of silks, perfumes and jewels. It was also filled with love and happiness. Nothing could have prepared her for the hardships of transportation across Soviet Russia — crammed into a cattle wagon with fifty or so other people in bitterly cold conditions — to the barren isolation of Kazakhstan. Many did not survive the journey; many did not live to see their homeland again. In this moving documentary, Eugenia Huntingdon recalls the harrowing years of her wartime exile.

FIREBALL

Bob Langley

Twenty-seven years ago: the rogue shoot-down of a Soviet spacecraft on a supersecret mission. Now: the SUCHKO 17 suddenly comes back to life three thousand feet beneath the Antarctic ice cap — with terrifying implications for the entire world. The discovery triggers a dark conspiracy that reaches from the depths of the sea to the edge of space — on a satellite with nuclear capabilities. One man and one woman must find the elusive mastermind of a plot with sinister roots in the American military elite, and bring the world back from the edge . . .

STANDING IN THE SHADOWS

Michelle Spring

Laura Principal is repelled but fascinated as she investigates the case of an eleven-year-old boy who has murdered his foster mother. It is not the sort of crime one would expect in Cambridge. The child, Daryll, has confessed to the brutal killing; now his elder brother wants to find out what has turned him into a ruthless killer. Laura confronts an investigation which is increasingly tainted with violence. And that's not all. Someone with an interest in the foster mother's murder is standing in the shadows, watching her every move . . .

NORMANDY SUMMER/ LOVE'S CHARADE

Joy St.Clair

NORMANDY SUMMER — Three cousins, Helen, Tally and Rosie, joined the First Aid Nursing Yeomanry. Helen had driven ambulances through The Blitz, but it was the Summer of 1944 that would change their lives irrevocably.

LOVE'S CHARADE — A broken down car, a mix-up of addresses and soon Kimberley found she was stand-in fiancée for a man she hardly knew. What chance had the pair of them of surviving this masquerade?